Timothy Shay Arthur

Our neighbors in the corner house

Timothy Shay Arthur

Our neighbors in the corner house

ISBN/EAN: 9783743303355

Manufactured in Europe, USA, Canada, Australia, Japa

Cover: Foto ©Andreas Hilbeck / pixelio.de

Manufactured and distributed by brebook publishing software
(www.brebook.com)

Timothy Shay Arthur

Our neighbors in the corner house

OUR NEIGHBORS

IN THE

CORNER HOUSE.

BY

T. S. ARTHUR.

———◆———

PHILADELPHIA:
JOHN E. POTTER AND COMPANY,
Nos. 614 AND 617 SANSOM STREET.

CHAPTER I.

"THE corner house is taken at last," said my wife one evening, looking up at me from her sewing; "I saw furniture going in to-day."

"I give the landlord joy," was my answer.

"You are thinking of the rent." My wife smiled.

"Yes. His interest on the investment will be light this year."

"While I am thinking of the tenants, and wondering what kind of neighbors we are to have."

"Woman-like," said I; "have you seen anything of them yet?"

"A carriage brought two ladies there. I happened to be at the window and saw the face of one of them as they alighted. It was that of a woman past middle age—thin, delicate in feature, with a cast of intellectual refinement. The other was in black, and deeply veiled. By her figure and style of dress, I should say she was young."

"Mother and daughter, perhaps," said I.

"That was my inference."

"In mourning? Probably a young widow."

"Or a young mother, sorrowing for the loss of her first-born."

My wife sighed; and I knew the meaning of her sigh. Our first-born was in heaven. Passing through the gate of death, he went thitherward, years gone by, while yet his life was fragrant with the innocence of boyhood. We did not mourn for him in black. Oh, no! our sorrow was too sacred a sentiment to be intruded upon others; and we could not shadow thus his rosy memory. Black for our baby? Oh, no, no! Anything but black! White were better, as symbolizing his angelic purity.

"Will you call upon our new neighbors?" I asked.

"Yes."

"From curiosity, inclination, or duty?"

"Each will have its influence. The strongest may be inclination."

On the next evening my wife had something more to say about our new neighbors in the corner house. There had been a second arrival in the person of a middle-aged man.

"What kind of a looking man was he?" I asked.

"I saw his face only for a moment. It did not impress me favorably. But faces in repose do not always give a right index of character."

"What was its peculiarity?" I asked.

"As I said before, I only saw it for a moment," replied my wife; "but think I should recognise it again anywhere."

"Then it must have been a strongly marked face?"

"It was. The types and styles of face that one meets every day are singularly varied; but not one in a hundred stands out so strongly from the rest as to hold the eye and picture itself on the mind as if the image had been taken by a camera."

"This man's face then belongs to the one in a hundred."

"Yes."

"Can you describe it?"

"I must see it again before I can particularize. What struck me was prominence of feature— prominent eyes, nose, lips, and chin."

"A sensual face."

"Sensual, but not animal. It was a strong face; and that indicates will and intellect of no mean order."

"Fair or dark?"

" Almost bronzed."

" You seem to have gathered something in that single glance," said I, smiling. " And this is all as to the new tenants of the corner house?"

" All that has yet appeared."

" Not all that will appear."

" No," answered my wife; " for I feel just curious enough to be observant, and I think there is a story in that corner house."

" There is a story in every house," said I, " and one to strike deep chords of feeling in the common heart if the right narrator could be found."

On the following day, as I passed the corner house, I glanced up at the parlor windows, the shutters of which were open. 'A face that was a perfect sunbeam met my vision. It was the face of a child lying close against the crystal pane. But another face drew my eyes almost instantly from that of the child. It was a little back in the room, and partly in shadow; but so white that it seemed ghostly. I saw it only for a moment in passing.

" Anything more from the corner house? " said I, on meeting my wife that evening.

She gave a quiet negative.

" I have seen the lady in black."

" What lady in black?"

" In the corner house."

" Oh! have you? " She was all interest.

"I saw her for an instant as I passed to-day. She was standing a little removed from the window, at which was one of the loveliest children I have ever seen. Her face was like alabaster—so pale and fixed; her eyes large, dark, and sad. If there had been warmth and feeling in her face, she would have been exquisitely beautiful."

"I wonder who she can be?" said my wife, visibly excited by my communication.

"The corner house has become to us a *terra incognita*. There will have to be a voyage of discovery," I remarked.

"My curiosity is so piqued, that I shall certainly make the voyage ere long," said my wife. "There was something in the step and air of this lady that interested me when I saw her alight from the carriage. I felt that there were passages in her life to draw strongly on a woman's sympathies."

"We must learn the name of this family, and something about them," said I, "before a call is made."

"The name at least ought to be known."

"And some facts in regard to the persons; as to their standing and reputation, for instance," said I.

"That would be satisfactory; but I don't think it probable that I shall delay calling for a very long time, should the antecedents of the family not appear. The face I saw, taking the face in repose as an index of character—your own theory—

was sufficiently indicative of a true woman to warrant friendly advances."

"It is well," I remarked, "to let prudential considerations have their right influence. If strangers make a mystery of their antecedents, the inference lies naturally against them."

"The mystery may refer to things over which they had no control. We must not wrong the individual, because unhappily the bad deeds of another have furnished his life with sorrow, and tainted the name he bears."

"If we know the truth, then we can act justly," said I. "It does not do to infer too much in regard to strangers, if our conduct towards them is to be governed by these inferences."

"If we suppose at all," replied my wife, "why not suppose good? If a stranger clothes himself with mystery, why not infer good of him instead of evil? The mystery may be a cloak to hide the conduct of others; and he may stand in need of our sustaining kindness, as he bends, almost fainting, under burdens that would crush the life out of you and me."

"This may all be so," I answered. "But let us look for a moment or two at the other side, and narrow down our suppositions to the present case. A family, of whom we know nothing, has moved into our neighborhood. There is a mystery about them; and where there is mystery, we naturally infer that something wrong or disgraceful has been done either by the individuals themselves, or by friends with whom they stood in intimate connexion. Now, let us take the lady in black at the corner house. You need only a glance at her ghostly face to be assured that at least one passage in the record of her life tells a fearful story. It may be that her hand is stained with blood."

"No!" exclaimed my wife, repelling the suggestion. But I saw the color fade from her cheeks.

"We cannot say yea, nor nay. Where there is mystery we are in the dark," said I. "Or, she may have been guilty of a crime that excludes her from virtuous society."

"I will not believe it!"

"For the sake of argument, I will assume it," I continued. "She has been guilty of a crime, and her family, seeking to veil her own and their disgrace, have withdrawn from the old social circles, and come to our city and neighborhood to hide themselves from observation. Take this for granted, and would you call upon the lady?"

My wife was silent.

"Would you call?"

I pressed the question, and got a woman's answer.

"I don't believe a syllable of what you infer."

CHAPTER II.

NYTHING new touching the corner house?" said I, half laughing, half in earnest, on the evening of the next day. I will confess that my curiosity was not altogether a passive element.

"Yes," replied my wife, "I have learned the name of its new occupants."

"Ah! so much gained. What is it?"

"Congreve."

"Not Jones, Smith, or Brown; but a name that suggests individuality of character, and an ancestry—good or bad. I am gratified to know that it isn't Smith or Jones."

"It is Congreve," said my wife, in a tone meant to rebuke my levity.

"How did you learn this?"

"Jane learned it from the grocer's boy."

"Perhaps the name is assumed," said I.

"Incorrigible man! What demon of suspicion has got access to your ear?"

"We know nothing about this family, Alice. They glide in among us unheralded, and throw around themselves a veil of mystery——"

I was going on quite earnestly, but she stopped me by saying :

"I am not aware that *they* have shown any mystery. *We* have made a mystery of their advent. That is all. No obligation rested on them as strangers to advertise the neighborhood as to who they were, or whence they came."

"Very true. I stand corrected. And so the name is Congreve? Did you learn anything beyond this?"

"The grocer's boy said they were from the South."

"The land of hot blood and quick-springing passion."

"There is hot blood and quick-springing passion everywhere," remarked Alice.

"True," said I.

"Then why speak of them in connexion with our new neighbors?" she asked.

"Thought clothes itself in speech, you know."

"But why should your thought take this direction?"

"Thought is a free rover. We cannot control its movements."

"Ah, well," said my wife, "I see how it is. Your impressions are against our friends in the cor-

ner house, and your thought runs in the same direction. As for me, I am going to infer good
instead of evil."

"And make them a neighborly call?"

"Yes."

At this moment our bell was jerked violently.
We both started, and then listened, while the servant went to the door. As it opened, we heard a
woman's voice. It was quick and excited. Then
rapid feet came along the passage and up the stairs.

"Won't you go into the corner house, ma'am?"
said Jane, pushing open the door of our sitting-
room.

"Into the corner house! Why should I go in
there, Jane?"

"You're wanted, ma'am. Something has happened; and the girl says please won't you come
in."

My wife looked at me in doubt.

"Go, Alice," said I.

She needed only a word of assent. There was
a moment or two of feminine adjustment of hair
and dress, and a glance into the mirror. Then
snatching up a netted hood, my wife glided away.
It was an hour before she returned. Her countenance was sober, and did not even light up with
its wonted smile as she greeted me.

"Such a scene as I have witnessed!" she said,
as she threw off her hood and sat down beside me.

I looked at her inquiringly, but did not speak. She drew a long, deep breath, and then went on:

" The child you saw at the window—a little sun-beam, truly!—was suddenly taken with convulsions. In the wild alarm that followed, a servant ran for some neighbor, and I happened to be the one summoned. I found her mother, the pale lady in black, sitting helpless, wringing her hands and uttering wild cries of terror; while the other and elder lady, whom I had seen alight with her from the carriage, was standing over the convulsed form of the child in distress and bewilderment.

" 'Oh, ma'am,' she said, eagerly, as I came in, 'where shall we send for a doctor? Is there one near at hand?'

"I turned to the servant who had come up stairs with me, and gave her the direction of our own physician. As she hurried from the room, I bent over the child. 'She is in spasms,' said I.

" 'She will die! she will die! Oh, can nothing be done to save my darling?' wailed the mother, in tones that thrilled you, they were so full of anguish.

" 'Bring a tub of hot water, quickly,' said I, to a domestic who was in the chamber.

" 'A tubful, ma'am?' she inquired.

" 'Full enough for a bath,' I answered. And she left the room immediately.

" By the time the servant returned, I had the

still convulsed form of the child ready for the bath, and lifting it in my arms, laid it tenderly in the water. How painful it was to feel the round soft limbs writhing and twitching, and to see spasm after spasm run over the sweet face of that little one. I held her in the water for more than ten minutes, and then laid her in the bed again. The more violent muscular contractions had by this time subsided, and there was some repose in her face. When Doctor Black arrived, she was still unconscious and in convulsions; but the worst symptoms had abated. He sat down by the bed-side in his quiet way, and after a few questions, and a few moments of observation, took out his pocket-case of remedies, and selecting a little bottle, dropped from it, between the lips of the child, a few of the white pellets it contained.

"Soon after I commenced bathing the little sufferer, her mother gained some control over her feelings, and, coming forward, asked in a querulous way what I was doing. 'The best that can be done until the doctor arrives,' I answered. She did not seem entirely satisfied; though the elder lady—her mother, I think—assured her that a hot bath was the right treatment for a child in spasms. 'Hasn't she been in long enough? Do take her out, won't you? Oh, dear! oh, dear! she'll die! Why don't the doctor come?' Queries and ejaculations like these were dropping constantly from her lips. When the doctor came in, her dark eyes fell on him with a glance of inquiry. He is a quiet, unobtrusive man, you know, and I understood in a moment that he did not impress her favorably. When he took out his case of medicines, and she saw the rows of little vials, she made a movement as if about entering a protest. But a hand was laid on her by the elder lady. The administration of a remedy was more than she could bear, and she broke out with an imperative—

"'I won't have my child doctored in that way!'

"Doctor Black arose and stepped a pace from the bedside. He was more disturbed than I had ever seen him.

"'It is *my* way, madam,' said he, with some dignity and some indignation, 'and if you don't wish me to treat your child, I can retire.'

"'We do wish you to treat her,' spoke out the elder. Then turning to the other, she said, in a firm, decisive manner: 'Edith, be quiet!'

"'You have been sent for, Doctor,' I now interposed, 'and you must not go without relieving the poor child of these dreadful spasms.'

"Doctor Black then resumed his place at the bedside, and taking the child's hand in his, laid his finger on the pulse, and sat noting its time and condition. At the end of ten minutes he gave another remedy. This was the signal for a second protest from the pale lady in black, who muttered, in a half-subdued way, her objection. I noted a strange gleam in her eyes as she fixed them on the doctor, and felt a low, unpleasant thrill pass along my nerves.

."No notice was taken of her, and the doctor gave up his entire thought to the little sufferer. The worst symptoms were now subsiding. The spasms occurred at longer and longer intervals, were of briefer duration, and less severe. After the lapse of ten minutes more, another remedy was given. The doctor observed its action for a little while, and then rising, said:

"'She is coming right, and will soon be as still as a quiet sleeper.'

"Then preparing two powders, he directed them to be dissolved each in a third of a glass of water, and a teaspoonful given, alternately, every half hour.

" He lingered yet for some minutes longer. His prediction came true. By this time every convulsed muscle had found tranquillity, and the face of the little one began to glow with warmth and beauty. Then the eyes unclosed, and the sweet lips, moving, pronounced the name of 'mother.' A scene of wild excitement followed, which came near throwing the patient into convulsions again. The undisciplined mother flung herself upon the bed, and in a strong burst of feeling, hugged the child to her bosom, and poured forth a torrent of fond words and a rain of tears.

"'Madam, for Heaven's sake, control yourself!' said Doctor Black. 'You will mar everything if you do not.'

"'Edith!' the other lady spoke almost sternly, 'do you wish to kill your child?'

"With a rebuked look, the mother disengaged her arms, and drew back, glancing from one face to another in a way that struck me as singular.

"'Give the medicines regularly, according to direction, and let nothing disturb our little patient,' said the doctor, as he moved towards the door. 'I will look in to-morrow morning, when I hope to find her quite well.'

"'He is a Homœopathic physician?' remarked the elder lady, as Doctor Black left the room. She looked at me steadily from her calm, brown eyes.

"I merely bowed an assent.

"'I have been taught to regard that system of medicine as involving absurdities of the grossest kind,' she continued.

"'Its professional opponents,' I replied, 'are not sparing in their denunciations. It is much to be regretted, however, for the sake of truth and science, that its imposing claims are not met by something better than denunciation and ridicule. You saw to-night with what singular rapidity the spasms subsided, after the administration of remedies that, to all appearance, had in them no potency whatever. Was it magic or medicine that wrought the salutary change?'

" 'I am not prepared to answer your query,' said the lady, with gentle dignity of manner. 'Our darling is better; and for this we cannot be thankful enough. It is God who cures—man is only his instrument.'

" 'To that sentiment do I, with all my heart, respond,' fell with earnestness from my lips. 'Every good gift is from God, and among these is the gift of healing.'

" As we talked thus, I noticed that the child was falling away into sleep. The mother observed it also, for her eyes were fixed on the little invalid's face. A shade of anxiety passed over her countenance, and she moved uneasily. 'Aunt Mary,' she said—I now understood the relation existing between them—speaking in a husky whisper, and looking anxiously at the elder lady.

" 'What, dear?' And the aunt leaned towards her.

" 'She's going to sleep!'

" 'So much the better,' was replied. 'There is more medicine in sleep than in any doctor's prescription.'

" 'But, aunt,'—she leaned closer, as if to prevent my hearing what she said—'maybe he's given her an anodyne.' The words reached my ears, for the whisper was distinct.

" 'Oh, no!' was replied.

" 'But, I'm sure they have,' she persisted. 'You know their medicines are very powerful.'

" 'Don't be in the least concerned, madam,' said I. 'They never give anodynes; and their medicines are not powerful in the way you suppose."

" 'But Doctor Jacoby told me that they were powerful, ma'am; that these Homœopathists, while pretending to give no medicines at all, actually gave more medicines, because in a highly concentrated form, than any other physicians living.'

" 'If Doctor Jacoby,' said I, warming a little, 'made that assertion, he was disgracefully ignorant, or something worse.'

" 'He ought to know,' said the lady.

" 'But it seems that he don't know; or, if knowing, is not veracious. Pardon my free speech, ma'am; but I must defend the right against all unfair assailants. Homœopathy can bear to have the truth alleged; and it is to the disgrace of its professional opposers that so many of them make false assertions in regard to its claims.'

"My earnestness did not call out any further remark. The elder of the ladies looked at me calmly, while I spoke; and I could not tell, by any play of her features, whether she took interest

in what I said, or had any faith in my strong assertions. As the child was now sleeping, I felt
that to remain longer might be an intrusion, and
so made a motion to retire. It was not opposed.
Thanks for the service I had rendered were expressed with warmth and sincerity, particularly by
the aunt, who held my hand tighter in hers for a
moment, and looked at me with a world of hidden
meaning in her face. But I was not asked to
repeat my visit."

"Well," said I, as my wife finished her story of
the evening's adventure, "you have penetrated
the outer court of this mystery."

"Mystery! What mystery?"

"Every individual life is a mystery. Every
household includes some mystery. And there are
secrets of the heart known only to God."

"True," answered my wife. "And in that
sense we are a mystery to our neighbors."

"Doubtless we are," said I. "Doubtless there
have been questions asked about us many times
which none answered satisfactorily, and which still
remain as unsolved problems. There is a penetralia in every family."

"The corner house includes a mystery in this
view of the case," replied my wife.

"And, as I said, you have passed the outer
court, and entered the vestibule."

"But did not reach the penetralia."

"What was the cause of convulsions in the child?" I asked.

"The cause was not stated. Doctor Black made some inquiries, but was answered with such evident evasion that he did not press the questions."

"That looks singular, to say the least of it," I remarked.

"It does. I felt all the while I was there as if something lay back of the condition in which I found the child, that did not and would not appear. No fall, sickness, over-eating, or fright, was even hinted at in explanation. There was a blank silence as to the cause."

"Where there is mystery like this, something wrong is evidently involved," said I.

"There is nothing wrong so far as the elder lady—Aunt Mary, as she was called—is concerned. You have only to look into her face to be assured of that. But there is something wrong in regard to the younger, who, pallid and ghastly as she appears, is yet singularly beautiful."

" Hers is a kind of weird beauty, I should say, judging from the partial glance I had of her face."

"You express the thing exactly," answered my wife. "It is a weird, and I should think, under some aspects, a fascinating beauty. The contrast between her and her aunt is remarkable. They are not, I should say, akin by blood."

"You saw no male member of the family?"

"None; but I am sure that I heard more than once, the sudden footfall of a man in the room above."

"Ah!"

"Yes; and I felt the more certain of this, from the fact, that the sound appeared to disturb Edith, as the sick child's mother was called. It came once when she was objecting to the treatment of Dr. Black, and I noticed that she halted for a moment in her words, and that a shadow flitted over her face."

"Well," said I, "the plot thickens, doesn't it?"

"We are to have a romance in the corner house," returned my wife, smiling, "if the present signs mean anything."

CHAPTER III.

D O you know anything about these people in the corner house?" asked our neighbor, Mrs. Wilkins, who had run in to chat with my wife an evening or two afterwards.

Alice said "No," and then asked Mrs. Wilkins what she knew of them.

"I don't know anything," replied our neighbor; "but there are some queer stories floating around."

"Indeed?"

"Yes."

"What is said of them?"

"Nothing outright, that I have heard, for people don't seem to know anything certain in regard to them."

"The queer stories," said I, "are then mostly in the shape of conjecture and inference."

"There's something hidden about them," replied

Mrs. Wilkins; " and anything like mystery, you know, sets people all agog to find out what is concealed."

" And when a whole neighborhood is on the alert and curious," I remarked, " it will go hard if something is not discovered.   But get a little nearer to terra firma—what is said about the people in the corner house ? "

" Well, now, let me see ! What is said? Oh, yes ? Mrs. Crowell says that, night before last, as her husband was coming by the corner house, about twelve o'clock, he heard a cry so sudden, wild, and startling, that it chilled for a moment the blood in his veins.   It was a woman's cry, and he is certain it came from that house.   There were no lights shining from any of the windows, and he could hear no movement within.   Then, the grocer-boy told our girl that they were the queerest people in the corner house he had ever seen, and that he believed there was something wrong."

" The grocer boy's opinion should not be taken in evidence against them," said I.

" Of course not," replied Mrs. Wilkins ; " but your grocer-boys, milkmen, and all that class of people, are sharp-sighted and quick at reading signs.   Their opinion of a family is not usually very far out of the way."

" And so the grocer-boy thinks there is something wrong ? "

"Yes; and he isn't alone in this opinion. It seems to be the common sentiment."

"That is the way of the world," said I; "something wrong is the first inference in all cases where people choose to hold themselves a little in reserve."

"People can't help their own inferences," replied Mrs. Wilkins.

"You mean," I answered, "that, as most people take a secret pleasure in hearing ill of their neighbors, when left to conjecture anything, they are very apt to let their conclusions favor the worst."

"Excuse me," Mrs. Wilkins replied, "but I will not admit your assertion that most people take a secret pleasure in hearing ill of their neighbors."

"It seems," said my wife, smiling, "that your own case proves your theory."

"My case! How?" I asked.

"Don't think me severe, but are you not judging very harshly of other people? As to the degree of pleasure you may feel in this judgment, it is not of course for me to speak."

"Fairly retorted!" laughed our neighbor.

"The homely old adage about measuring other people's corn by our own bushel, is pleasantly illustrated in your case. Is it from the secret gratification you experience when ill is told of a neighbor, that you form your estimation of others?"

Mrs Wilkins grew quite animated. Her eyes sparkled.

"There may be something in the suggestion," I said. "Human nature is sadly depraved. Even you have brightened up wonderfully, in making the supposed discovery that I am quite as bad as I make out my neighbors to be."

"Come, come!" was replied; "This is fighting at too little advantage on either side. We shall both get damaged, I fear. It is far safer to lie in ambuscade, and shoot our arrows without the danger of retaliation."

We were sitting in our parlor. I had noticed a faint ringing of the street door bell, and heard the servant pass along the hall. There was a question from a woman's voice; a rustle of garments; a light step—so light that the ear scarcely noted the sound. We glanced to the parlor door expectantly, and the white face of our neighbor in the corner house looked in strangely upon us.

"Mrs. Congreve!" said my wife, starting quickly forward, and taking the hand of our unexpected visitor. She advanced, with a hesitating step, across the room, Alice leading her towards Mrs. Wilkins and myself. I arose, and with all the blandness of manner I could assume, gave her a welcome to our house. But she was not at ease;

and glanced, in a furtive way, now at me, and now at Mrs. Wilkins—at the same time that she drew close to my wife, beside whom she sat down on a sofa. Her dress was black in every part; and this gave to her colorless face and hands a ghostly whiteness. About her lips, on which rested an expression of unutterable sadness, there was a slight, but constant motion; and her eyes, that were large and round, were as restless as her lips. I saw in a few moments, that she had not expected to see any one but my wife, and that the presence of both Mrs. Wilkins and myself was a source of embarrassment. Mrs. Wilkins also saw this, and with a self-denying thoughtfulness very creditable under the circumstances, when a woman's proverbial curiosity is taken into account, excused herself, and went home. I was then about to retire from the parlor, but my curiosity tempted me to remain a little longer; and as the lady seemed to be now more at ease, I resumed the chair from which I had arisen on the departure of our neighbor.

"How is the little one?" now asked my wife.

"Florry? oh, she's well again."

What a mournful voice it was! From what far-off places in the mind did its low, sad echoes, come back!

"Was she ever in that way before?" asked my wife.

"No; but wasn't it dreadful!" And I could ee that the remembrance caused a low shudder to creep through her nerves.

"She may have eaten something that was not readily digestible," said I.

The large, strange eyes looked into mine for a moment or two; but there was no response to the suggestion.

"I have noticed, several times, the face of your little Florry at the window," I remarked. "It is a very sweet face."

Something meant to be a smile played over the dead blank of her countenance as I said this; but she did not reply. Ill at ease she was. I saw this plainly enough. It was evident that she had come in to see my wife alone; so, after one more fruitless effort to get her interested, I excused myself and left the room. I saw at a glance that my departure was wholly agreeable to our visitor. But, scarcely had I reached the family sitting-room, when a loud jangling of the door-bell startled me. I went to the head of the stairs and listened.

"Is Mrs. Congreve here?" I heard, in a woman's voice, followed by the exclamation? "Why, Edith! How could you do so?"

A few low words followed, and then the street door shut, and my wife stood alone in the hall. I went down to her quickly.

"Who came for her?" I asked.

"Her aunt."

"What did she say?"

"Nothing beyond an exclamation of surprise and relief. But she looked pale and frightened."

"More mystery," said I. "What can lie at the bottom of all this?"

"Mrs. Congreve is not in her right mind; of that, I think there is little doubt."

"But what has disturbed the even balance of her intellect? I would give something to know."

"Women are proverbially curious," said my wife, in a meaning way.

"You forming an exception in this case," I retorted.

"Perhaps not," she answered, quietly; then added, "Insanity, you are aware, runs in some families. It may be hereditary in the case of Mrs. Congreve."

"Yes, it may be."

"Though you doubt it."

"You indicate my state of mind."

"On what do you base a doubt?"

I had nothing tangible to set forth, and so only shook my head.

"Did she say anything after I left the room?" I inquired.

"She was about making some communication," replied my wife, "when the appearance of her aunt checked the words on her lips. She listened to your departing steps with almost anxious intentness, and as soon as you were at the head of the stairs, turned to me, every muscle of her face quivering with interest, and her lips apart to speak. But she started as the bell rang, and a shade of fear went over her face, when the voice of her aunt was heard at the door.

"'I must go,' she said, rising with a disturbed manner. And I heard her murmur to herself: 'They watch me as if I were a criminal trying to escape!'"

"If her aunt had only kept away a little longer," said I, "we might have obtained the clue to this mystery."

"Which you are dying to penetrate."

"No, not in that extremity. But——"

"Suffering from a tantalizing curiosity. I did not expect this of you. But, there is the bell again. What next."

It was only Mrs. Wilkins. She had watched from her window opposite, and seeing Mrs. Congreve depart, came over to hear what she could. We had nothing satisfactory to communicate, to her evident disappointment.

"It's my husband's opinion," she said, as she sat, talking on the subject, "that there is something about these people that will startle the neighborhood when it comes out—if it ever does. There is not a good look about Mr. Congreve. Mr.

Wilkins says that he has met him several times in the neighborhood or coming out of his house; but has not once been able to catch his eye. It's his opinion that Congreve is not his real name."

"What has suggested this?" I asked.

"I'll tell you what," she replied. "A merchant from the south-west was in his store one day this week, when Mr. Congreve happened to pass. The man started as he saw him, and half uttered, in a tone of surprise, some name different from Congreve.

"'Do you know that person?' asked my husband. The man answered, 'I presume not. It is only a striking resemblance.'

"'His name is Congreve,' said Mr. Wilkins. 'He is a stranger in our city, from the south, I think.'

"The man repeated the words 'from the South,' as if struck by them; but added; 'I don't know him,' and changed the subject."

"Singular," I remarked.

"Isn't it? My husband thinks the man knew him, and had motives for concealing the knowledge."

"Possibly. It looks as if it might be so."

"More mystery," said my wife, smiling.

"And this may be the clue. Did your husband say from what town in the south-west the merchant came?"

"He did not."

"Of course he knows."

"Without doubt, as the man was a customer."

"Any circumstance that would make a family exile itself from an old home or familiar neighborhood, would in all probability become a matter of public notoriety. Another customer from the same town may be able to throw light on the whole subject. Suggest this to Mr. Wilkins."

"You are right. I'll do that," replied our neighbor, with animation. "It will be strange, if we don't get to the bottom of this mystery before long."

CHAPTER IV.

THE shutters of the corner house were bowed from parlor to third story, as I passed on the next morning; bowed when I came home at dinner-time; and bowed at evening twilight. My question: "Anything more from the Congreves?" was answered by a quiet shake of the head.

On the next day, the house gave no more intelligible sign; and no more on the next.

In the evening, Mrs. Wilkins came in. I saw, the moment she entered, that she had something to communicate. After sitting for a little while, she said:

"My husband had another customer in from N——, to-day, and it occurred to him to ask if there had been any strange or startling event in his town, recently, or within a year or two. The man didn't remember that there had been any unusual occurrence, when first questioned; but afterwards told Mr. Wilkins a sad story about the young wife of a planter, who had become infatuated with an Englishman. The husband's suspicions becoming aroused, he watched them with untiring jealousy; and, at last, discovering what he regarded as proofs of guilt, shot the lover in the presence of his horror-stricken wife. The planter was arrested, tried for the murder, and acquitted. Immediately, he sold his estates and left the neighborhood with his family. The wretched woman who had caused this fearful disaster lost her reason, and was sent, he thinks, to one of our northern asylums. The event caused great excitement at the time."

"Did your husband ask the name of the family?" I inquired.

"Yes; and it was not Congreve. But, for all that, I think they are in our neighborhood."

"Have you any ground, beyond mere conjecture, for this belief?"

"Yes. My husband described Mr. Congreve, and the Southerner thought he must be the man. He had not seen him many times; but as far as he could remember him, the identity seemed clear."

"I don't believe he is the man," said my wife, in a tone that caused me to turn and look into her face. She was pale and agitated.

"I am sure of it," replied Mrs. Wilkins. "That

lady in the corner house is deranged. You have only to look at her to be assured of this."

"Her reason may be unsettled; but not by guilt." (My wife spoke confidently.) "I know a pure face when I see it—a pure face that reflects a pure mind—and this you have in Mrs. Congreve."

"Oh! as to that," said Mrs. Wilkins, "her husband's blind jealousy may have imagined guilt where none existed. But she must have been strangely imprudent for a pure woman. When a wife gives countenance to a lover, innocence dies in her heart. Poor child that she was!—her beauty bartered for gold; bartered ere the girlish sweetness of tender seventeen had put on a woman's thought and feeling—no wonder that, when her heart's true impulses came into vigorous life, they drew her aside from virtue."

"You speak confidently," I remarked.

"The story that my husband heard recited the case as I give it. She was very beautiful, and gold won the prize that many strove for eagerly. The rich planter, twice her age, and repulsive in person and appearance as another Bluebeard, bore her away to his home in triumph. But the young singing-bird soon lost her voice in the gilded cage and narrow apartments that now imprisoned her. The happy-hearted girl changed quickly to the sad-hearted woman. A few wretched years of a false life, and then a falser life began. There was no altar in her heart on which love's pure flame could burn; and so passion built a place on which to sacrifice to other gods than those which preside over domestic peace. Her feet got bewildered in strange labyrinthine paths; she lost her way! Unhappy child-woman! We pity more than we blame."

"Your picture, faintly outlined as it is," said I, " gives me a shudder. Whether your gold-bartered southern child-woman be our neighbor or not, she is a burden-bearer, whose stooping shoulders let the too heavy weight of remorse or anguish of unblessed love fall crushingly upon her heart. Somewhere she sits in darkness—somewhere suffers—somewhere looks with fear into the black, hopeless future. Alas, for that blindest, that maddest of all follies, which sacrifices a heart on the altar of mammon! Are there not wrecks enough for warning on the shores of every sea?"

"It would seem not," replied Mrs. Wilkins. Then added, following my own thought: "The maddest of all follies indeed! The heart of a woman, that loving thing, so wonderfully sensitive to all influences, and with such infinite capacities for joy or pain; so hard to indurate, though it lie for years in the petrifying waters of worldliness and sin; so tender and yielding to love, so passionate in revolt. A woman's heart! Oh, with what care should it be guarded! Yet, how is every door of evil influence opened upon it ! It is assailed by pride, love of the world, wealth, and all *blinding* influences, before a true self-consciousness gives token of its own inherent wants, capacities, and powers. Alas! that this knowledge comes in so many cases too late; that bonds which dare not be broken, have fettered it ere the first yearnings for true freedom are known. And of all bonds, these golden ones usually cut deepest into the palpitating flesh; for where gold is the power that binds, you rarely have the manly qualities that a true woman must recognise ere love can spring to life in her heart. A bought slave cannot be held by affection; she will feel her fetters, no matter how costly may be the material, and seek to trample them under her feet."

Alice had remained silent since her simple rejection of the supposed identity of Mrs. Congreve and the southern planter's wife referred to by Mrs. Wilkins. I glanced now and then at her face, and saw that it retained the shadow which had suddenly fallen over it.

"It is not well," she now said, in a voice that was unusually sober, "to take anything for granted in a case involving so much as this. Let us not prejudge and ill-judge these strangers on no better evidence than yet appears."

"The presumptive evidence is very clear," remarked Mrs. Wilkins.

"Not to my mind," was answered. "Any other set of circumstances might be made to appear just as conclusive against them. I'm afraid we are all more inclined to think the worst instead of the best, where any question or doubt exists. The rule that gives to a prisoner the benefit of a doubt, is sensible and humane."

Mrs. Wilkins had gone home, and my wife and I still talked of this new aspect which had been given to the case of our neighbors in the corner house, when a servant came to the room in which we were sitting, and said, in a hurried way:

"The girl from Congreve's is down stairs, and wants to see you, ma'am, right quick."

My wife started up at this summons, and ran down to the hall in which the girl was standing. I heard a few quick, eagerly spoken words pass between them, and then my wife called to me in an alarmed tone of voice.

"What is it?" I asked, as a few long strides brought me to the foot of the stairway.

"We are both wanted in at the corner." And my wife grasped my arm in a nervous manner.

"What for?" I inquired.

"Heaven knows! But get your hat and come quickly. The girl looked pale with fright."

"Where is she?"

"Gone! She flashed out as if half beside herself."

I caught my hat from the rack, and hurried away with my wife. The door stood partly open, and we entered the corner house without ringing for admittance. I noticed, as my eye glanced into the parlors, that the furniture was scanty, rather than in profusion; and plain rather than elegant. The woman, whom I knew only as Aunt Mary, stood a few steps below the landing on the stairway, with a face of ashen paleness.

"Here! Quick! quick!" she called, as soon as we entered.

I sprang forward, and as I commenced ascending the stairs, she turned and flew up the next flight, and was at the door of the front chamber when I reached the upper landing.

"Quick!"

I was by her side in an instant.

"She's fastened herself in with Florry; and I can't get a word from her or hear a sound."

I understood, from the white terror in her face, that she was in fear of the worst that could happen; and so threw myself against the door with considerable force. But it did not yield.

"Edith! Edith!" called Aunt Mary, in wild fear.

But, though we listened, holding our breaths, no sound came from within that deathly silent room.

Again I assaulted the door, but from the firmness with which it withstood the shock, I felt sure that it was bolted as well as locked.

"Has the door a bolt?" I asked.

"Yes," came in a husky whisper.

"Have you an axe?" I spoke to the girl.

"Yes, sir."

"Fly, fly for it!" exclaimed Aunt Mary, throwing her hands forward to give force to the injunction. Then looking into my face, she murmured, in a fluttering voice, "She's dead, dead! I'm sure of it!"

"Let us all throw ourselves against the door at once," I suggested. "It may yield."

And in the next moment it gave way to this united assault. The fumes of burning charcoal filled my nostrils as I stepped into the room, and I cried out:

"Stand back, on your lives!"

Receding as I spoke, I bore back the two women, Aunt Mary and my wife, who were about entering with me. The room was in darkness; but I saw, indistinctly, two figures lying on the bed.

"Remain here," I said, imperatively, "until I can get the windows open."

Then, holding my breath, that the deadly gas might not enter my lungs, I dashed across the room, and threw open the sashes and shutters. As I turned, I saw on the floor an ordinary clay hand-furnace, in which the red coals were still burning. Snatching this up, as I sprang back towards the door, I removed it from the room.

"Bring some cold water, instantly," said I to the servant, as I handed her the furnace.

It now occurred to me, that the surest way to save the lives of Mrs. Congreve and her child, if the fatal work she had sought to accomplish were not already done, would be to remove them from the room. The thought was scarcely half formed in my mind, when I crossed to the bed, and lifting little Florry, reached her light form to my wife. Then going back, I gathered the slender, and to all appearance lifeless body of the mother in my arms, and bore it from the room also.

Side by side we laid them in the adjoining chamber. What a sight to be remembered it was! The pale face of Mrs. Congreve was a little darkened by congestion; but it was serene as the face of one who slept, dreaming peaceful dreams. Her black garments had been laid aside, and in their place she wore a snowy muslin night-dress. Her hair, which lay smoothly parted away from her delicate, feminine forehead, had been drawn behind her ears and knotted low down upon her neck, with womanly care. The act had evidently been soberly premeditated; and the preparations conducted with deliberation. Florry was also in

her night-dress. Her countenance, like that of
her mother, was slightly congested, but showed n
mark of suffering.

CHAPTER V.

DIRECTED water to be dashed into their faces. The effect was more than I had hoped. for. A slight gasp followed the shock; and there was a nervous quivering along the neck and about the lips and nostrils of both.

"There is life remaining," I said eagerly. "Send for a doctor."

"Can a doctor give help now?"

The aunt laid her hand on my arm, and looked at me meaningly. I understood her, and turning to the bed, placed my fingers on the wrist of Mrs. Congreve. As I did so, I noticed that her hand was tightly clenched upon something. It was several moments before I could find the lowest motion of life; but it came, an almost imperceptible beat against the sensitive fingers. Was I in error? Had hope and imagination deceived me? No!—there it was again!—softer and feebler than a new-born infant's—now with two or three almost fluttering waves; and now again in a single throb after a prolonged cessation. Then I laid my hand over the heart of dear little Florry—my eyes grew dim as I looked into her death-hued face. There was no mistaking its muffled beat. I bent down my ear. Yes, she breathed!

"Thank God that we were in time!" I murmured, rising up. "Ten minutes longer, and no human power could have saved them."

"Must the doctor be called?"

"Wait a little. Perhaps they will revive without his aid."

Even as I spoke, there came a deep sigh from the lips of Mrs. Congreve, followed by a low sound, like a groan. Water was again thrown into both their faces; and this time with much effect. Florry began to show many signs of returning animation.

No one seemed to have noticed the clenched hand of Mrs. Congreve but myself. As I stooped over her again, I saw the edge of a narrow piece of blue ribbon between her closed fingers. Aunt Mary turned away from the bed for some purpose, going to a distant part of the room. Curiosity, even in this dreadful hour, was strong. What was in that hand, clutched and clung to in the very death-hour? My hand was on the woman's insensible hand; I pressed back the fingers—they yielded, and my eyes rested on the miniature of a young man; rested for a minute only, but long enough to recognise the face! Suddenly, the fingers of Mrs. Congreve closed again, tightly, on the medallion, and she turned her pale face towards me, which, though the eyes were still shut, showed half-consciousness and feeling.

The pure air which had been passing into the lungs of little Florry, and giving back life again to the exhausted flood, now began to inflate them in fuller volume. Consciousness was restored. Rising up, she looked at us from her large blue eyes in a questioning, frightened way.

"Take me, Aunty," she cried, stretching out her hands.

Aunt Mary caught her up from the bed, almost smothering her, as she did so, with kisses.

"My precious, precious one!" she murmured, in a low, sobbing voice, and then bore her from the room.

"Aunt Mary!" called Mrs. Congreve, now sitting up in bed, and looking first at me and then at my wife, strangely and in sad bewilderment of thought. "Where is Aunt Mary?" She threw her eyes, half-wildly and with an expression of alarm, about the room.

My wife bent over her and said, in a tone meant to dispel anxiety and alarm :

"She will return in a moment. Lie down again. You are weak and sick."

"Sick, did you say?"

Then her eyes fell suddenly to the hand which still clasped the miniature. She opened it, but shut the fingers again with a nervous quickness and hid the hand instantly in her bosom. When it was withdrawn the palm lay open to sight. I glanced at my wife, and saw by her startled eyes and the paleness of her cheeks, that she had seen the pictured face which had been a little while before revealed to my wondering vision. Feeling now that my presence was no longer required in the room, and could only be embarrassing, I withdrew without a word. I met Aunt Mary as I came out into the passage.

"How is she?"

"Recovering rapidly," I answered.

"The doctor will not be required?"

"No."

"I am glad of that." Then she stood silent for a little while.

"Don't go yet, sir. I would like to have a few words with you after seeing Edith. Will you remain for a short time?"

I promised to remain, and went down stairs to the parlors, where the gas had been lighted. I felt greatly excited. The miniature in the hand of Mrs. Congreve—showing me a face I never could forget—was a new mystery. Where did she get that miniature, and what to her was the unhappy man it represented with such life-like fidelity?

CHAPTER VI.

I SAT pondering, conjecturing, and guessing, but with no satisfaction to myself, when my wife came down stairs, accompanied by the aunt of Mrs. Congreve.

This woman was small in stature, of light frame, and with delicately cut features. Her eyes were of a dark hazel—you might take them for black at the first glance—and her complexion fair, and her skin of a pure, pearly transparency. Her nose and forehead would have given a fine Grecian outline, but for the slight aquiline rising of the former. Her chin advanced instead of receding, and rounded into something like a voluptuous fulness, that gave you rather the idea of self-reliance than even a suggestion of sensuality. Grey tokens of years or suffering mingled in many silvery lines amid the masses of her glossy brown hair. Thought, endurance, self-conquest, and pain had all been at work on her face—at work for years; but they had not cut away a line of that true womanly beauty which is of the soul. They had abraded the flesh, only to let the spirit shine through with less obstruction. Her step had in it a dignity that made you feel yourself in the presence of one who had risen above all life's meaner things.

I arose as she entered the room. But she said, in her low, evenly-modulated tones:

"I must keep you here a little while longer; so, pray, be seated again."

"How is Mrs. Congreve?" I inquired, as I sat down.

"Safe from the danger that threatened her life, and sleeping."

"It was a narrow escape," said I.

"Fearful to think of!" And the lady shuddered.

"Has she ever attempted her life before?" I asked.

She looked at me half in doubt, I could see, for a little while before answering, and then said, with undisguised reluctance:

"Yes."

I regretted having asked the question. Aunt Mary—for so I must designate her as yet—felt embarrassed by my query. This was plain.

"I must," she said, looking up into my face— her eyes had been resting on the floor—"ask of you one thing; secresy, for the present at least, in regard to what you have seen to-night. No good can arise from bruiting this frightful circumstance. And it will be painful to us in the extreme to have it noised throughout the neighborhood."

"You have nothing to apprehend on that score," I answered quickly. "I can speak both for my wife and myself."

She gave me her hand from a grateful impulse, saying:

"I thank you sincerely; you make me twice your debtor."

"Think of us," I said, "as your friends, and call upon us freely for any service in our power to render."

Her hand, that still lay in mine, closed with a gentle, confiding pressure, and was then withdrawn. I was touched by her tone and manner; so quiet, and yet so full of feeling.

"Mr. Congreve is away?" said I.

"Yes." She answered no further. The tone was different from that of a moment before.

"Can we serve you in anything more?" I asked.

"Not to-night," she replied.

"Do you think," inquired my wife, "that it will be safe to leave her alone?"

"Oh, I shall not leave her! I sleep always in the same room."

I saw that she was very pale, and was beginning to show considerable repressed nervousness.

"If you would care to have me remain with you all night, ma'am," said my wife.

"Thank you for the kindness of heart that suggests the offer; but I will not tax your good-will so far."

I saw, that even while she declined the overture, it was in her heart to accept of it.

"My wife is entirely in earnest; I can speak for that," said I. "Had you not better take her at her word?"

Aunt Mary looked irresolute. My wife arose, saying,

"I do not think it well for you to be left alone to-night. This dreadful occurrence has shocked you severely. I know you want a friend, and I will be to you, for the present, that friend. In half an hour I will return, and stay until the morning."

"May He who gives, with every kind impulse that flows into the heart, a blessing, bless you, my stranger-friend. I will not refuse what I so much desire. Come!"

There were tears in her beautiful eyes as we turned away and left the room.

"You saw that minaiture?"

It was my first remark, as we sat down alone together, after reaching home.

"I did."

"And recognised it?"

"Yes."

"How comes it in her possession? What has she to do with him?"

"I am in a maze," replied my wife.

"Had he become entangled in any love affair at the time of his fall?" I asked.

"I think something was said about a marriage engagement. Yes, I remember now. And it was reported that the young lady shut herself up from society for a long time afterwards."

"Evidently Mrs. Congreve knew him then, or since his release from prison; and this sad condition, in which we find her, is referable, I am sure, to some relation between them."

"The miniature," said my wife, "gives us his face of ten years ago—not the face he must wear since that dreadful ordeal through which crime forced him to pass. Have you heard of him since he came out of prison?"

"Not a word."

"He was pardoned out, I think."

"Yes. Some extenuating circumstances were urged upon the Governor, and some false swearing of witnesses alleged, I believe. At any rate, the unhappy young man was sent back into the world again. What became of him I never learned."

"You remember the story Mrs. Wilkins told us a little while ago?"

"Yes." I felt a chill creep along my nerves.

"He may have been murdered by Mr. Congreve!" The blood went back from my wife's face.

"That is too terrible to think of! No, I will not believe it."

"But why, when seeking to destroy her own life, did she hold that miniature in her hand?"

"I cannot say, Alice. There is a fearful mystery—tragedy, I fear—connected with her life."

"And we have the clue to it in that miniature. Poor Edgar! Who would have thought that, ten years ago, when all the future looked so bright and beautiful before him, when his praise was on all lips, that, in a little while, his feet would stray from the right paths, and his sky, all so blue and sunny, grow dark with tempest and ruin? He fell suddenly from a mountain-peak, and was bruised, past sound recovery, I fear, in the fall. Unhappy young man! How often the thought of him has given me the heart-ache. His poor mother went down with the shock. But she, true to her mother-love, always said he was innocent."

"His own assertion."

"Yes. He claimed to be the victim of a conspiracy."

"And may have been. Heaven knows, I would rather believe that than guilt. But never was evidence clearer against any man."

My wife returned to the corner house, to stay with Aunt Mary, and I retired for the night to sleep fitfully, and with disturbing dreams, or lie in wakeful puzzlings of the unquiet brain, until day-dawn.

Alice came in very soon after sunrise. She looked pale and weary, like one who had passed the night in watching; but had little to communicate that reached an answer to the many questions pressing on both of our minds. She sat up with Aunt Mary until nearly twelve o'clock, talking; not, however, on any subject connected with the mystery that surrounded the family.

"There is something about her," said my wife, "that attracts like a magnet. I never met any one to whom I was drawn so powerfully. Her mind is rarely endowed; and she has a way of looking at things that shows her to possess a deep religious trust."

"She has need of such a trust," I suggested.

"And this very need, it strikes me, has given birth to a faith that lifts, amid storm and darkness, its steady eyes upwards."

"Did she make no allusion to herself, or to her niece?" I asked.

"No direct intelligible allusion."

"What did you talk about?"

"Not so much of the outer as of the inner world; not so much of events as of mental states and conflicts. I noticed often as we conversed, forms of speech, views of life, and admitted experiences, that showed not only close thought and observation, but a profound knowledge of the human heart. She is no ordinary woman. And to think of her, shut out from circles of refinement and intelligence; hiding away from observation, and her life darkened by a mystery that is struggling for concealment, makes the heart sad."

"The very qualities she possesses are doubtless needed," said I, "to grapple with this mystery, and destroy, in the end, its power. There is no form of human evil that has not its counterbalancing good; no disease without an all-potent remedy. In His infinite adaptations of means to ends, God acts with unerring wisdom, and unfailing love. If she is the true woman you think, God has given her a work to do which no selfish, shallow weakling could perform. She may pass the days in pain now, but there shall follow a season of rest and peace in the time to come, when He makes up His jewels."

"Her mind struck me as breathing in a serene atmosphere now," replied my wife, "as dwelling in a house which, though beaten upon by the rain, and made to shudder in the wildly rushing winds, rested firm on its rocky foundations. There was nothing of a complaining or despondent spirit about her; but a brave lifting up of the heart and a steady eye in advance. Some of the sentiments which she uttered in our conversation, struck me as exceedingly beautiful; and they were given in words most fitly spoken. I have hardly met with her equal, as a woman of cultivated mind, and rare powers of conversation."

"The night passed without any further excitement, I suppose," said I.

"No; as we sat talking in the room next to that in which Mrs. Congreve was sleeping, we were startled by a low, wailing cry, so full of inexpressible anguish that my heart stood still and shuddered. Aunt Mary started up, and I followed her rapid feet as she passed to the adjoining chamber. Mrs. Congreve was sitting up in bed, with a face of ghastly whiteness, and her eyes distended and protruding fearfully.

"'Oh, Aunt Mary!' she cried, falling forward, and hiding her face in her aunt's garments.

"'What is it, dear? What has frightened you?' asked Aunt Mary, in a gentle, soothing way. 'You have been dreaming.'

"'Was it a dream?' The poor lady's voice was calmer, yet not fully assured. 'I thought he was here, and—and—'

"She glanced at me, became silent, and seemed, I thought, embarrassed. Aunt Mary did not reply to what she said. With a long, sad sigh, Mrs. Congreve fell back again on her pillow, shut her eyes, and turned her face to the wall.

"'You must be tired and sleepy,' said Aunt Mary, rising from the bed and turning to me. 'I have not been thoughtful in keeping you up so late. Bless me! It is nearly one o'clock.' She had drawn out her watch. 'Come, I will show you to your room.' And she led the way to a small chamber on the same floor.

"'Don't hesitate to call me, if I can be of any service,' said I, as she turned to leave me. 'I am not a sound sleeper; your lightest tap at my door will bring me wide awake.'

"'There will be no occasion for disturbing you, I trust,' she replied, as something like a smile lighted up her gentle face. 'Good night, and God bless you!'

"And no occasion came, if I am to judge from the fact that, after turning restlessly on my bed for two hours, unable from excitement of mind to lose myself in unconsciousness, I sank away to sleep at last, and did not wake until the morning sun looked in upon my face and drew me back from the land of dreams."

CHAPTER VII.

THE miniature we had seen in the possession of Mrs. Congreve, was that of a young man named Edgar Holman, a cousin to my wife of the second remove. From boyhood up to the time he attained his twenty-third year, he had borne an unblemished character. For over five years before going to the West, which removal took place when he reached his twenty-first year, he was a steady and welcome visitor to our family, and I had become warmly attached to him.

Madison, Indiana, was the point to which he removed, and we soon had intelligence from him of the most gratifying character. He was clerk in a large mercantile establishment, at a fair salary, and in a position where good conduct, united with ability, and the qualities he possessed, were sure to advance him in the world. Now and then, a letter came from him in which he spoke cheerily of his prospects.

I was sipping my coffee and reading the newspaper, one morning, when a paragraph met my eyes that sent the blood coldly to my heart. It ran thus:

"SERIOUS FORGERY.—A young man named Edgar Holman, in the employment of Fairfield & Co:, Madison, Indiana, has been arrested on the charge of forgery. The evidence, in a preliminary examination of the case, looks conclusive against him. The amount obtained on a forged check was over three thousand dollars. The circumstance has made a profound sensation in the community where it occurred, as the unhappy young man bore an unblemished character, and had the unlimited confidence of his employers."

"What's the matter?" asked my wife, who sat opposite to me at the table, and noticed a change in my countenance.

"Bad news, Alice," I replied.

"Bad for whom? What is it?" she inquired, a slight shade of alarm falling over her face.

"Edgar has been arrested on the charge of forgery!"

"Impossible!" She grew deadly pale.

I lifted the newspaper and read aloud the painful announcement.

"His poor mother! It will kill her!" said my

wife, as the tears flooded her cheeks. "But is there not some mistake? Is the name really that of Edgar Holman?"

I looked at the fatal paragraph again. The name stood out in unmistakable distinctness; and we knew that he was in the employment of Fairfield & Co.

"I read it to you as it stands here, Alice."

"I cannot believe it!" she said. "There is some error. Edgar is not the one to throw character, happiness, everything a man holds dear and sacred, to the winds, for a few thousands of dollars. No, no! Depend upon it, he is the victim of some strangely lying circumstances, and his innocence will appear."

"God grant that it may be so!" The words came chokingly into utterance. I remembered this sentence: "The evidence in the preliminary examination of the case looks conclusive against him."

"He is in His hands," said my wife, meekly.

"Yes; and if his cause is just, justice will, in the end, prevail."

"And yet," replied Alice, the troubled tone coming back into her voice, "there have been many cases in which innocence has borne the burden of guilt."

"That is so. In most cases, however, innocence stands justified in the end, and the tried soul comes forth, in its white garments, more saintly for the ordeal; and if more saintly, who will affirm that, no matter what of the earthly has been consumed in the fire, the ordeal was not a blessing instead of a calamity. There are natures in which the gold is so intimately blended with some baser metal, that only the intensest fire can sever the connexion."

"A hard doctrine," said my wife.

"Sin makes a necessity for many hard doctrines. If there had been no sin there would have been no suffering. Sin transmits its evil proclivities, and but for God's providence, that, in wise ordainment, brings adequate reactions upon our perverted desires, we would be carried by them to destruction as surely as the leaf is borne away on the bosom of a wildly rushing stream."

"But," said my wife, "if Edgar is innocent of this crime, for which he stands charged, what possible good can arise from such a blasting of all his worldly prospects; such a staining of his fair reputation; such a hell of suffering as he must of necessity endure?"

"If innocent, not a hell of suffering," I made answer. "Only the evil are in hell. You must find some other term. In Bedford jail, falsely accused, cast out from his fellow men, and cut off from hope in the world, good old John Bunyan was not in hell. No, no. That poor prison on the bridge, with its narrow, comfortless walls, must often have been as the very gate of heaven to his soul. There is an infinite difference between the pain of those who suffer for well-doing, and of those who suffer for evil-doing. Keep that always in mind. It is something on the side of consolation."

"Something on the side of consolation! A straw cast to a drowning man! Think of yourself under such an accusation as now stands against that poor young man!" My wife spoke with a flushing face, and tremulous but half-indignant tones.

"No, not a straw, but a beam of wood, to save the wretch from sinking. If I were under such an accusation, would not self-conscious innocence be a sustaining power? Could any force of the current sweep me wholly away or drag me under? Would not my life be safe?—the life of my soul?—innocent life? It would be safe, Alice! The storms might rage, and the floods lift themselves against me; but they could not prevail."

"Oh, to some, what a troubled dream is existence!" was exclaimed as I ceased speaking. "To some, what crushing burdens have to be borne! To some, how strangely tangled becomes the skein of life! I cannot see it clear! There must be an error somewhere "

"Only in our estimate of things seen but in part; not in the last results. Good is superior to evil, and its final conquest is as sure as day-dawn after the solemn midnight. Not every spirit is vital enough with the elements of heavenly life, nor strong enough in immortal fibre, to bear the fierce trials that are needed to bend the hard nature which lifts itself in conscious pride and selfhood, and even while confessing God with the lips, rejects him in the heart. Such a rejection is fatal to happiness. We are not self-existent; have no life, except what flows into our spiritual organism; cannot draw a single breath except through power received from the Author of our being. Yet so perfect is the appearance of thinking and acting from ourselves, that we are all the while in danger of falling into the error of Lucifer, son of the morning. Pride whispers in our ears a pleasant suggestion of self-originating power; and our hearts begin to beat with a fuller measure. We have but to will, and from the all-creative will must spring the means of compassing our ends. We become as gods in the world; each for himself —each grasping after its good things, and each looking upon them as most to be desired for blessing. Now that infinite love which desires to lift us out of this darkness and error, which can only lead us to eternal unhappiness, is united with infinite wisdom and prescience; and in providing for the correction of our errors, so orders, or permits, our way in the world, that the circumstances we encounter shall react upon and help in the correction of destructivo evils. Only God can know what are the required circumstances; for only He sees what is in the heart, and how it will respond to correction. As for us, we can only be patient, and wait for the good time which will surely come, if in our patience we hold fast to our integrity."

"Poor boy!" said my wife. "There could not have been in him any evil requiring such a discipline as this."

"That is," I replied, "assuming his innocence. But he may have fallen in an hour of temptation; may have put forth his hand, as the allegation assumes, and laid it covetously upon what belonged to another."

"The thing is too improbable. I will not believe it," she answered. "He is the victim of lying circumstances."

"Will you go and see Mrs. Holman?" I asked.

"Yes; I must go there. Oh, dear! I turn sick at the thought of meeting her."

"Give her my earnest sympathy, and say that whatever I can do in this unhappy case shall be done with all my heart."

My wife found Mrs. Holman in a state of sad

prostration.   Two days before, she had received a letter from her son, informing her of the dreadful charge which had been made against him.   " I can only say, dear mother," he wrote, " that I am as innocent of the crime as when I lay an infant in your arms, and I know you will believe me. Whether I can make my innocence appear on the trial which I shall have to stand, is known only to Him who looks into all hearts.   There is a strange agreement in the evidence which has been brought against me.   Even the teller at the bank swears that, to the best of his knowledge and belief, I am the person to whom he paid the check.   He says that he knows me by sight well, and has been in the habit of taking from me the checks of the firm, all of which is true.   A part of the money, which he swears to be of the same denomination as the notes paid to me on the forged check, was found on my person when I was arrested, and in my pocket-book!   Moreover, two half-filled up checks and a sheet of paper written over with various imitations of Fairfield & Co.'s signature, were found in my desk.   And yet, to make the case still stronger against me, by an additional circumstance in the chain of evidence, the salesman of a jeweller swears that I bought of him a gold watch for eighty dollars on the day the forgery was committed, and paid him in bills of the bank on which the check was drawn.   These bills are produced, and prove to be twenties, the denomination of the bills sworn to by the teller as having been paid to me. I am thus explicit, dear mother, in order to prepare your mind for the worst. A dark conspiracy to ruin me has been laid; but by whom, and to what end, I am not only ignorant, but unfurnished by even a suspicion. At present, I have no defence except my asseveration of innocence. But as, in cases of this kind, the guilt of an accused party is usually a foregone conclusion in the public mind, this will avail me nothing. I try to keep a brave heart in this fearful calamity—try to believe that God will make my innocence appear. But it is impossible to contemplate the worst that may come, without a shudder."

I give only that portion of his letter which speaks of his relation to the crime charged against him.

When the trial of the case came on I was in attendance. The best counsel was employed; and I had gone over with them, carefully and anxiously, all of the case and evidence which could be reached before coming into court for defence. They did not present a very hopeful aspect. I found a strong feeling in the community against my young friend. Everybody seemed to regard him as guilty. The case was set down as clear for conviction. "I would be one to lynch a jury that would render a verdict of not guilty," I heard a man say while the subject was discussed in his presence. I mention this to show how strongly set the tide of public sentiment. In my own mind conviction wavered. I found Edgar greatly changed. He had fallen into a depressed condition of mind, and looked wretched and despairing. He declared himself innocent; but it did not seem to me with the confidence of an innocent person. I was not assured by his manner; and had more doubts, after seeing him, than before. Still I hoped that on the trial something would occur to change to a more favorable aspect the look that things wore.

At last the day of trial came. The court-room was crowded almost to suffocation. Edgar took his place as the accused, looking pale and haggard, but with firm lips and steady, watchful eyes. I did not see much change in his countenance, while the prosecuting attorney recited the case as it stood for trial, and stated the points he relied on competent witnesses to prove. The evidence was then called. It was clear, coherent, and hung together as witness after witness took the stand, and gave testimony in a chain that I could see forging to bind the unhappy young man in disgrace and ruin. To my own mind his guilt was established; and as I looked at his miserable face, tears of pity made my sight dim.

For the defence little was attempted. At the

hour, according to the teller's evidence, the check was drawn, it was proved that Edgar was away from the store, and he failed to show where he was at the time. The teller was called upon to describe the dress worn by the party to whom the check was paid. He designated a shawl and cap which other witnesses swore answered exactly to a shawl and cap worn by Edgar. The wearing of this shawl and cap on that day Edgar denied. It was a clear sunny day, and these were only worn by him in very cold or stormy weather. In order, if possible, to get something on the favorable side here, a clerk from the store of Fairfield & Co. was called to the witness-stand, and questioned as to the fact of these articles being worn on the day in question by Edgar. He remembered the day well, and was certain the prisoner had on that particular cap and shawl.

The case went finally to the jury after a feeble effort on the defensive side, and in less than half an hour the wretched young man's ears were stunned by the verdict of "Guilty."

CHAPTER VIII.

T would be hard to forget that day, and that scene. Clear as was the evidence against Edgar Holman, plain to all eyes, as it was, that the jury had little question of his guilt when they left the box to deliberate on a verdict, I yet saw hope in the wretched young man's face when he was brought into court by the officer who had him in charge, to hear the verdict. A dead blank of hopelessness I had rather seen; for then there could be no shock of feeling to a lower depth. The cup would have been full, the circle of fire complete, the pain half deadened by its accumulated intensity.

When the Judge directed him to stand up and hear the verdict, he caught, with nervous eagerness, at the railing by which he sat, and drew himself to his feet. There came a flush upon his wan face, and I could see his eyes gleam as he turned them upon the foreman of the jury, on whose first utterance hung his fate. Too soon, also, came the fatal word. As it struck harshly upon the still air, it staggered him like a heavy blow. The faint flush went out from his face like the sudden extinguishment of a taper. I never saw such a face before, with a live heart beating in the bosom beneath. How was it that he had dared to hope? Yet it was plain that, in spite of the mountain-weight of evidence which had been brought against him, he had looked for a different result. Could it have been anything more than the hope of a felon, who stretches his eyes eagerly beyond the crowd assembled to see the last tragedy in his life enacted, in vain expectation of a reprieve? I know not; but this result, which all had looked for, found him alone unprepared. His head sank forward after a moment of statue-like stillness, and he drooped down into the chair from which he had just arisen, apparently unconscious of what was passing around him. The Judge directed his removal to prison, there to await sentence of the law.

On the next day I was permitted to see him. He was greatly changed. The restless nervousness which had shown itself before the trial, was gone. He appeared like one who had been stunned by a shock, from the effects of which he still suffered. No reference was made to the trial or verdict. I did not speak of it, and he omitted even the remotest allusion thereto. What could I say to him? Oh! words had nothing in them for such a case. I believed him guilty, and he could not but have seen it. What an embarrassing interview it was!—embarrassing beyond anything I had ever known.

On the following day he was sentenced to seven years' imprisonment at hard labor in the State Prison; and all men said the sentence was just. I saw him once again after the sentence, and for the last time. The dead stupor that fell upon him at the rendition of the verdict, which cut him off from hope, had passed away, and his mind was clear and calm. Once only did I refer to his position, as a man convicted of crime, in the remark, that I trusted the few years of expiation that lay before him would do a salutary work. His eyes flashed instantly, and he looked at me with a gaze of such fiery intensity that I turned my face partly aside.

"You will see my poor mother," he remarked, in a failing voice, as I was about leaving him.

"Yes. What shall I say to her, Edgar?"

"Only this from me—*that I am innocent.*"

He did not take his sad eyes from mine even for an instant, as he said this.

"Nothing more?" I asked, after a pause.

"Nothing more," he replied, in a mournful

voice. "They are the only words of comfort in my power to send. She will believe them."

And so I parted from him. Yes, his mother believed them. In her eyes he was innocent, though to all else he was guilty, and the law exacted, in stern retribution, the penalty of guilt. But faith in her son could not give strength sufficient for her day of trial. In less than a year after his imprisonment she passed to her everlasting rest.

Five years of the term allotted to him were served out by Edgar, when in some way, the particulars of which did not reach me, interest was made for him with the Governor of the State, who granted a pardon.

All the circumstances of the case were brought back vividly to my mind, by the singular fact of his miniature being found in the possession of Mrs. Congreve.

"You were satisfied of his guilt," said my wife, as we talked over the matter a few days afterwards.

"Not a doubt of it crossed my mind after listening to the evidence adduced at the trial. And yet the expression of his face, and the steady gaze, and almost fiery flash of his eyes, when I assumed as a settled thing his guilt, at our last interview, have often been remembered, and not always without a question as to what they really meant. Were they assumed to impress me for his

mother's sake, or were, they the signs of innocence?"

"Let us believe them the signs of innocence,"
said my wife, a new interest in her unhappy
relative awakening in her mind.

"And, as a consequence," I answered, "take to
my troubled consciousness the fact that I turned
from him coldly, in the hour of his greatest extremity, with my judgment of the case adding its weight
to the crushing burden that lay upon his heart.
I don't like to think of that, Alice. I was almost
his only friend in that darkest time of his life;
and when I turned from him and left him to his
fate, how the blackness of midnight must have
fallen around him! Innocent! No, Alice. He
was not innocent. The thought almost suffocates
me."

"Better innocent—better a thousand times!"
answered my wife. "The suffering of guilt is
a hell, down into which no white-robed angel
comes with words of hope and comfort."

"True—true. Yes, better innocent—better a
thousand times! It is now nearly two years
since his release from imprisonment?"

"Yes."

"And we have heard nothing of him since that
time?"

"No."

"Was it not said that evidence in proof of

some false swearing on the part of witnesses was brought to the Governor?"

"Yes. We heard that."

I let my thoughts run back over the intervening seven years, and recalled, as distinctly as possible, the several witnesses. There was one of these who gave his name, I remembered, with rather an unseemly interest in his affirmations, as if he were particularly desirous that his evidence should be conclusive against the prisoner. He it was who testified to the fact of Holman's having worn the shawl and cap by which the teller identified him. I noticed his appearance at the time, and was affected by it unpleasantly. But the idea of a perjured witness did not cross my mind. Now the circumstance began to have a significance. This young man might have committed the forgery himself? I could not find, however, much to sustain the hypothesis; and soon dismissed it from my thoughts.

"We shall get lower down into the heart of this matter before long," said my wife.

"Through our strange neighbors in the corner house?"

"Yes."

"And uncover, it may be, a tragedy that might better sleep. You have not forgotten the story told by Mrs. Wilkins?"

"I am not willing to believe in the story—

not, at least, as applied to this case. It is so short a time after his release from prison, Edgar could not have become thus involved."

"As the story goes, it was a young Englishman. He might have assumed that character by way of disguise."

But my wife would not give the suggestion any credence.

Two or three days passed without our seeing or hearing from the Congreves. Mrs. Wilkins, whose curiosity had become greatly piqued in regard to them, and whose dwelling was so situated that she could keep the corner house under surveillance, came in almost every day to see my wife, and, as she supposed, compare notes. But the showing of notes was all on her side. My wife had gained so much of a personal interest in the family, to say nothing of her promise to Aunt Mary, that her own lips were guarded with jealous care. She received all that Mrs. Wilkins had to give and kept her own discoveries to herself. But Mrs. Wilkins had nothing of interest to communicate. Two or three times she had seen Aunt Mary go out and come in. A few parcels had been left. Once an express-wagon stopped at the door, and a large box was delivered. And there had been at least two telegrams to somebody in the house; she knew this must be so, for a boy had handed in a little book, with a letter, on both occasions, and received back anwers.

"That telegraph business," said Mrs. Wilkins, "looks to me suspicious. Two dispatches to a private house, in two consecutive days—and there may have been a dozen. I could not watch all the while, you know—it is not a usual circumstance, by any means."

"Did you see anything of Mr. Congreve?" asked my wife.

"No, not a sign of him. And that's a little singular."

Every circumstance becomes magnified into singularity where suspicion is an admitted guest.

"I have my own notions about him," added Mrs. Wilkins.

"What are they?"

"I don't believe he is away from home."

"Why do you doubt his absence?"

"It's just my opinion that he is within them four brick walls at the corner, hiding away in dread of discovery."

"Then you will have him to be the murderer of that young Englishman."

"I believe it in my heart."

My wife did not attempt to remove this impression. It was to her a most painful view of the case—painful, as involving Mrs. Congreve in the charge of infidelity, but significant of the fate of her cousin.

"I've seen a suspicious-looking man loitering about the neighborhood, and especially near the corner house, for several days past," said Mrs. Wilkins. "Once he walked up to the door and rang the bell. I would have given something handsome to have heard what passed between him and the servant who came to the door. It was plain that the answer she gave to his questions did not satisfy him, for he stood talking to her for some time, and once, after going partly down the steps, returned to say something more."

On the third evening after the nearly fatal attempt of Mrs. Congreve to take her own life and that of her child, Alice ventured upon a call. She had said to Aunt Mary, "Be sure to send for me if I can serve you in anything." But Aunt Mary had not sent for her during this period, and she did not feel free to intrude herself. Now, however, a sufficient time had passed to admit of a friendly visit without the appearance of any curious interest, which all persons occupying an equivocal position must feel as annoying. I own to having awaited her appearance with a certain degree of restlessness which I could not overcome. Her countenance wore its usual quiet expression when she came in. I saw at a glance that nothing had occurred to excite her mind, or to answer the questions we were both so anxious to solve.

"How did you find Mrs. Congreve?" I asked.

"Very different from the state in which I found her on my previous visits. She was calm, gentle, and lady-like in her manners; though for much of the time silent. I did not see anything of the wildness displayed on the occasion of her sudden appearance here; nor of the restlessness and querulousness I had once noticed. Indeed nothing occurred to indicate a disordered mind. She was singularly pale, as when I first saw her, and the sadness of her mouth and eyes was not once, during the evening, softened by a smile. Aunt Mary was lovelier than ever. So gentle, so sweet, so intelligent. Such noble views of life! Such a profound trust in Providence! Once, as Mrs. Congreve expressed a doubt in regard to all things being adjusted for our highest good, Aunt Mary said, with a countenance full of divine confidence—'Though He slay me, yet will I trust in him.'

"Mrs. Congreve shook her head in a doubting manner, and turning to me, said:

"'Aunt Mary's faith exceeds mine, as well as her patience and resignation. She is one of those who can kiss the hand that holds the rod. I am not as submissive, however. She looks through every dark cloud, and sees sunshine above; through every high mountain that lies across her path, and sees green fields and pleasant rivers beyond. All will come out right. That is the anchor of her soul. Ah, if I could only think so—only think so!'

"Her voice grew mournful—she sighed deeply—her eyes fell to the floor, and she sat very still.

"'Aunt Mary is right,' said I. 'God's providence acts by unerring laws. There can be no miscalculations where infinite intelligence directs in the affairs of men.'

"She turned her eyes upon my face with a strange, questioning look, and said:

"'Where innocence is cruelly struck down—when a fair name is blighted by falsehood—when the pure and honorable are made to bear the expiation that is demanded for crime—do you say that there is no miscalculation?'

"She grew excited; I saw her eyes dilating, her lips arching, and her thin nostrils beginning to widen. But now Aunt Mary leaned towards her, and laying her hand upon her restless hand, said, with a most loving tenderness, and a smile that an angel's face might have worn—

"'Don't wander away, darling, into this maze of doubt! It 'will all grow clear, clear as noonday. Night only endures, in any life, for a season.

There is a golden morning to break over the mountains; and its time is sure.'

"Mrs. Congreve looked steadily into the face that bent near her own, as if she understood it to possess a magical power. And verily I believe it did, for her perturbed spirit. The fluttering heart soon folded its startled wings, and settled down quietly in her bosom. She did not speak again, except in some casual remark, but sat busily knitting, with her eyes, for the most part, on the work in her hands."

"You stayed late," said I.

"It was because the time glided pleasantly away in Aunt Mary's company. I scarcely noted the passing moments. There is a spiritual beauty in her character not often seen. She is gentle and wise. A true lady, because a true woman. I could sit and listen unwearied to her true words for hours, and come away stronger for duty and humanity."

"These states of aberration, on the part of Mrs. Congreve," said I, "are not permanent, it would seem."

"No; her condition to-night shows that."

"Did you not think her remark about innocence being struck down, and a fair name blighted by falsehood, singular under the circumstances?"

"I was struck by it. Evidently, she believes

Edgar to have been the victim of a base conspiracy," said my wife, "and doubtless she is in possession of facts unknown to us. I will accept her view, and believe him innocent. But where is he? And what is his relation to this heart-stricken, unhappy woman? These are questions that grow more and more clamorous for solution every hour."

"We must wait for a while yet," said I. "The clue is in our own hands, I think, and time will bring us to the heart of this mystery."

CHAPTER IX.

"YOUR visit has been a very pleasant one," was the remark of Aunt Mary, as my wife rose to go home.

"Not more pleasant to you than it has proved to me," answered my wife.

"Will you come again?" Aunt Mary's eyes gave warrant of her sincerity.

"If my visits will be agreeable."

Aunt Mary took her hand, as she replied:

"They will always be agreeable. You have been very kind and very considerate—more like a true-hearted friend than a stranger. Come and see us often, if you will waive the formality of a full return of visits. I will repay what I can."

My wife accepted this friendly overture, and made frequent visits to the corner house; always growing more and more interested in both aunt

and niece, who proved to be highly educated, re-
fined, and intelligent.

Several months had passed since this family
entered our neighborhood, yet were we, apparently, no nearer a solution of the mystery that surrounded them, than when the first intimations
came of their being in some way involved with
our cousin. For nearly three months of this period we had seen nothing of Mr. Congreve.

One evening, my wife, who went in often, sat
talking with Mrs. Congreve and her aunt, when a
man's step was heard in the passage below. An
exclamation came from the lips of Mrs. Congreve.
Alice looked towards her, and saw that the face
was agitated, and the expression strange—almost
fearful. Rising, she passed from the room with
swift, noiseless steps. Aunt Mary did not move
nor show any unusual disturbance. Her face was
partly turned aside, so that it could not be clearly
seen. A heavy step moved along the hall, then
ascended the stairs. Aunt Mary now arose, and
half crossed the room to the door. It was Mr.
Congreve.

"This was the first time I had met him," said
my wife, in relating the circumstance; "and the
first opportunity for observing him closely. His
face, as you know, is strongly marked; a prominence of feature being one of its peculiarities.
His complexion is quite dark. I thought him, as

he stood in the door, with the light of feeling in his countenance, a handsome man, but not a good man. Strength, will, passion, were clearly indicated, and not only these, but disappointment and suffering.

" ' Aunt Mary,' he uttered her name in a kind of dead level tone, as though he had returned after an hour's absence. She did not offer him her hand—I noticed that—nor give him a welcome word. But her voice was gentle and kind as she presented him to me, and pronounced his name. He came into the room and sat down, addressing me a few words in a courteous manner, though he was by no means at ease in my presence. I sat as long, after he came, as seemed right under the circumstances, and then returned home."

Scarcely had my wife ceased speaking, when some one gave our bell a desperate jerk, and she started to her feet. She was nervous about the effect on Mrs. Congreve of her husband's return, and this sudden loud ring unsettled her.

"Mrs. Congreve, as I live!" she exclaimed, as she bent over the baluster. Then she went flying down stairs. I followed. My wife had drawn her into the parlor, and they stood together, the arm of Alice around her, as I entered.

"My husband," said Alice.

I bowed, but my appearance was not welcome.

I saw this, but kept my ground. There were signs of deep disturbance on the face of Mrs. Congreve. My wife drew her to a sofa, and sat down, holding both her hands. After several minutes of silence, Mrs. Congreve said, in a husky fluttering voice, "You must forgive me, friends, for this unseemly intrusion." She looked at me and then at my wife. I sat down in front of them. The word friends included me, of course, and I accepted the recognition. There was nothing of that wild incoherence of manner seen on the occasion of a similar visit made some months before.

"Does Aunt Mary know of this?" asked my wife.

Mrs. Congreve shook her head.

"It will frighten her."

"I can't help it. You will let me stay here to-night?" and she looked with appealing earnestness into my wife's face.

"On one condition," replied Alice, promptly.

"What?"

"You must send word to Aunt Mary that you are here."

Mrs. Congreve thought for some moments.

"I will write her a note."

"Very well."

I brought paper and a pencil. The note was hurriedly written, and my wife conveyed it herself, as we did not wish to let our domestics into the secret of what was passing any further than could be helped. Mrs. Congreve sat without speaking a word until her return, and I did not think it wise to intrude any remark.

"Did you see her?" she asked, with evident anxiety, when my wife returned.

"No; I gave the note to Jane, and told her to be sure to place it in Aunt Mary's hands."

For the next three or four minutes she sat listening, as if every moment in expectation that some one would appear. Then she breathed more freely, and showed signs of relief.

"I think," she now said, speaking in that tone which is assumed in reverie, not looking up into our faces, "that I must be living in a dream. This can't all be real! Is it real, or is it phantasy?"

She lifted her eyes to the face of my wife, and gazed at her in a doubting, curious way.

"If real," she added, "then fact is stranger than fiction."

"The real," replied Alice, "is the actual of our inner lives; the enduring things, their quality. Change, mystery, doubt, wrong, sweep around us in the ever mutable external—but the inner life is secure, if we wisely make it so. In the maze of circumstances by which we are involved, we seem at times to be dreaming. We ask ourselves, as you do now, am I sleeping or awake? Is it real or a phantasy ? In part, it is phantasy. We look at the bewildering investiture of external circumstances until their true meaning is lost, and we give them a significance that misleads us. But this is not wise. Let us go down into our hearts and see to what measure they beat. Let us lay aside covering after covering, and get at their true quality. Let us see whether God's laws are our laws."

"Laws—laws—" She looked bewildered. "The heart is bound by no laws. You cannot trammel *it* with fetters. The heart is free."

" Only in true freedom when bound by the laws of God," said Alice, calmly. " Blind passion and evil impulse are not freedom."

" But is there not freedom in true love ? "

She fixed her eyes with an intensity of inquiry on the face of my wife.

" If love," was the answer, " makes a false vow ; if it binds itself with solemn pledges, against which the heart rebels, the bonds are self-wrought, and may not be broken. Love is not free in this case."

The hands of Mrs. Congreve were laid slowly over her bosom, and I saw them press tightly against it, as if she were attempting, by an external act, to still the disturbed beating within.

" It is a mystery," she sighed. · " I cannot see it clearly. Aunt Mary talks so ; and she is good and wise. You talk so, and I think you good and wise, also. But it is hard—hard, I cannot bear it, I am not strong enough."

"But you will be," said my wife, confidently. "Time and God's Providence are at work. You have been made to pass through a region that must have been dark and fearful as the valley of the shadow of death; but there is a plain way for your feet; and delectable mountains, from which the eye can see beyond the enchanted ground, even to the eternal city, whose walls are of jasper, and the buildings thereof pure gold, clear as crystal. Move on, steadily, bravely, like old Christian; ever looking upwards for strength and comfort. All must come out right in the end. God will surely bring it to pass."

Mrs. Congreve bent towards my wife, and looked at her wonderingly.

"Has Aunt Mary told you?" she asked, almost in a whisper.

"Told me of what?"

Mrs. Congreve drew away, like one conscious of having unwittingly half betrayed herself. There succeeded a long pause, in which I withdrew from the parlor. Soon after, they followed me, but passed the sitting-room and went to my wife's chamber. In about twenty minutes Alice came alone, and said that Mrs. Congreve would sleep that night with her.

"I would not feel safe," she said, " to leave her

in a room alone. Aunt Mary always sleeps with her."

This I thought but common prudence. She stayed with me only a few minutes, and then went back to Mrs. Congreve. I slept in the room adjoining, and, for full two hours after I was in bed, heard the low murmur of voices; or, rather, for the most part, of a single voice, which I knew to be that of our visitor.

The eyes of my wife, when I looked into them on the next morning, were full of mysterious intelligence.

"I have such a story to relate!" she said in a half whisper.

"Of Edgar?" I asked.

"Yes."

"He has not been murdered?"

"No—no. He is living, I trust, and, what is best of all, innocent!"

"Thank God for that! But where is he?"

Alice shook her head. "It is not known."

"Did you tell her that you knew Edgar? That he was your cousin?"

"No; I kept this concealed. Was I not right?"

"I think so."

The sound of Mrs. Congreve's step in the passage, as she came out of the chamber where she had passed the night with my wife, was now heard, and Alice left me to join her. We met at the breakfast table. I read the face of Mrs. Congreve with curious interest, as she sat nearly opposite. I had only seen it in the gas-light before, except in a casual glance as she stood at the window of her own house. Her deep black made its whiteness unnatural. She looked very young; even with the signs of suffering so strongly impressed on every feature, not over twenty-five. Her eyes were large, clear, of great depth, and singular beauty. When the light of a happy heart was in them they must have charmed and bewitched almost every beholder. The style of her face was not strictly classic; but, while very pure and delicate, with something more passionate than is seen in the Grecian outline, her mouth did not express strength of character. You saw that feeling would rule, under strong excitement, even against reason. So the face impressed me.

She said very little during the meal, and ate scarcely anything. It was plain that she felt herself in an embarrassed position, as far as I was concerned. And no wonder.

On my return at dinner-time I found Mrs. Congreve still an inmate of my house. I learned from Alice that Aunt Mary had been in, and tried in vain to persuade her to go back.

" Not while he is in the house! " was her resolute answer.

Still Aunt Mary urged her niece in her gentle,

earnest way, using arguments founded on duty and high religious obligations, when Mrs. Congreve exclaimed, passionately,

"I will not go back! I hate and loathe him! His very name is an offence to me!"

Fearful that her mind might be thrown again from its equipoise, it was thought best to permit her, for the present, to have her way. She did not come from her room at dinner-time. My wife gave me a few passages from the long history to which she had listened during the previous night. They made my ears tingle. The full narrative I give in succeeding chapters, related in the words of Mrs. Congreve herself.

CHAPTER X.

F I am not in a dream, life is indeed a fearful thing—that is, my life. Sometimes I persuade myself that I am only dreaming; that a nightmare is resting on me, and I try to arouse myself. But I still dream on in the same wretched way.

I had another dream once—I will call it a dream, for there came a sudden and wild awakening. Oh, it was a sweet, sweet, delicious dream of heaven on the earth! But I am losing myself. I want to talk to you of my past life; to tell you a story that will give you the heart-ache. Shall I go on?

My father was a physician in the West. Where, I will not say now. I was his only child, and he was very ambitious in regard to me. Every advantage of education was afforded, and every possible accomplishment sought to be engrafted. The discipline of my girlish life was severe enough to diminish much of its enjoyment. But I had a quick mind and buoyant feelings. These prevented the breaking down of my spirits under a pressure of tasks that were not portioned out by my teachers with any kind of judgment or discretion.

When I was twelve years old, my mother died; but her place was supplied to me by dear Aunt Mary, her sister, the wisest and best woman that ever lived. In my nineteenth year I came home from school, having completed the course of education assigned to me. My heart was free, as it had always been. There was hardly a girl of my age in the Academy, who had not, either in sport or earnest, encouraged a lover. But my fancies did not run in that way. Young men, at least those it had been my fortune to meet, were not, in anything, up to my ideal of the sex. I had an ideal. Not one dwelt upon in waking dreams, however. It was more an unconscious than a fondly cherished ideal. I can say that up to this period of my life I had seen in no man's face anything that gave my heart a quicker motion—anything that I felt as a peculiar attraction—anything that dwelt with me hauntingly when alone. Yet was I conscious of a deep capacity for loving. There was in my thought faintly imaged, a home, in which I dwelt as in a kind of earthly paradise; a home such as I had never seen, yet had faith in as a possibility. There was no selfish worldliness in this home; but the concord of all sweet affections.

My father was a man whose hard struggle with life had made him set an undue value upon wealth as a means of happiness. I think that in educating me with such care as he evinced, the leading thought in his mind was my preparation for what he would consider an advantageous marriage: money and position being regarded as the chief prerequisite. I can only account for this blindness of judgment in a man who saw so clearly in most cases, in the way just intimated. His long struggle with poverty, and the pains and disabilities thereby entailed, caused him to magnify riches as the highest attainable earthly good; or, rather, as the means of reaching all good the world had to offer. His education and high professional standing made him a man of rank in the community, and naturally singled me out, and gave me a certain distinctive position when I entered society. My beauty—the homage of admiring eyes, the image in my glass, the words not spoken for my ears that reached them, all told me that I was beautiful—added to other and higher attractions of the mind, soon drew a crowd around me. There was more than one of these to whom my father would have given his daughter in marriage, without a sign of hesitation.

One day, a few weeks after my return home

from school, as I sat at the window, looking out into the flower-garden that lay in front of our small but tasteful dwelling, I heard the gate open, and casting my eyes down the walk, saw a young man enter and approach the house. Something in his face, as our eyes met, held my gaze, until he passed from sight under the vine-covered portico. As he rang the bell, my heart gave a little bound, and then fluttered strangely for a moment. My father's office was on the other side of the hall. I sat listening, until a servant opened the door; and then I heard the young man enter and go into the office. In a few minutes he came out, and I heard the front door shut. I looked from the window, and saw him move down the walk. After passing through the gate, he paused to close it, and in doing so, turned his face towards the window at which I was still seated. Our eyes met again, and again mine rested in his, until he turned from me and walked down the street. I did not attempt to withdraw my eyes; and I doubt if I possessed power to do so. Again my heart gave a little throb, and again fluttered in a strange, new way..

At this instant I heard the office door open quickly. My father came out, crossed the hall, and looked into the parlor. He did not speak, but I saw his brows contract a little, as his eyes rested upon me steadily, and I thought with a shade of suspicion in them, for a prolonged moment. I was conscious that my cheeks grew suddenly warmer, and that my manner lost its quiet self-possession. He went back to his office without speaking.

It was plain to me that my father had seen the young man pause and look towards the parlor window, and that he had left his office to see if I were sitting there. This fact bound the other fact in my mind, and gave it a more distinct impression; and, at the same time, I felt, painfully, that I was not to be left free in any matter of the heart. I had already discovered a certain worldliness, as it then struck me, in my father; a looking to wealth and social standing as higher than personal qualities.

"And am I to be sacrificed to these!" said I, as I sat that day at the window, with my eyes upon the little gate through which the stranger had passed, and, in passing, left his image in my mind. And, then and there, I said, resolutely, "Never!"

At dinner-time I discovered, two or three times, in looking up suddenly, my father's eye fixed intently on my face, and each time I was conscious of a heightened color. Naturally enough, I connected this unusual scrutiny of my countenance with the incident of the morning, and so the incident was kept more vividly in thought.

All at once I seemed awakening to a new consciousness. When my head went down upon its pillow that night I was not the same being in all things who had arisen from quiet dreams in the morning. An inner world, in which I moved vaguely, I saw, indistinctly, had opened upon me. I felt an indefinite yearning after something that included the happiness of my life; and with it came a fear that this something would for ever elude my grasp. I had passed from girlhood to womanhood in a single hour!

I can never forget that first night of my new consciousness. I slept and awoke many times— the hours lapsing away in wakeful musings, or sleeping dreams—sweet, weird, bewildering phantasies, that haunted me long afterwards with their delicious memories.

On the next morning, as we met at the breakfast-table, I saw that the new interest in my father's mind had not died out. I was changed in something, and it was plain to me that he saw it. My usual vivacity was gone, and so was my usual keen appetite.

"Are you not well, Edith?" asked my father.

I tried to smile indifferently as I answered that I was very well; but the expression of my face by no means satisfied him. He looked uneasy and concerned. As he arose from the table at the conclusion of breakfast, he came around to where I was sitting, and laid his fingers on my wrist.

"Your pulse beats rather quickly," he remarked. "Didn't you sleep well?"

"Not very well," I replied.

He scanned my face closely, and then left us and went to his office to attend to some patients who had called. From the breakfast-room I passed to the parlor, and sat down at the window over-looking the garden at the front of the house. Usually I practised on the piano immediately after breakfast; but I felt no desire now to touch the instrument, although I was extremely fond of music, and had acquired considerable skill as a performer. I had taken a book from the centre-table and laid it open in my lap, but not to read, so quickly was I learning the art of concealment. In a little while Aunt Mary—she had lived with us since my mother's death—came in and lingered, talking for some time. How I wished she would leave me alone! It was the first time in all my life that I had felt her presence an unwelcome one.

"Don't you feel well enough to practise?" she asked, coming to the window, and laying her hand on my shoulder in her affectionate way.

"Oh, yes, I'm well enough," I answered; "but the practising humor is not on me this morning."

Just then I heard the gate-latch click. Looking up, I met the face that had haunted me since yesterday. I did not stir nor speak until it passed from sight beneath the portico, and the distant tinkling of the door-bell came to my ears.

"I must say a word to that young man," re-marked Aunt Mary, leaving the window and going quickly from the parlor. For a short time I heard them speaking together in the hall, in what seemed a familiar way; but nothing of what they said came to my ears. Then I heard him go into my father's office, and Aunt Mary's footsteps sound on the stairs as she ascended to the rooms above.

"She knows him!" The words moved, in a whispered ejaculation, on my lips.

It was full ten minutes before the young man left my father and passed from the house. He moved with quick steps down the walk, opened and shut the gate, then stood on the outside, and looked towards the window at which I was seated. Our eyes met as on the day before. There was no sign of recognition on his part; nothing like a smile, or shade of presuming familiarity; but a half wonder, blended with admiration, in his eyes, and a deep seriousness on his handsome countenance. What he read in my face I could not tell, for I was unconscious of what it expressed. He stood, as it seemed to me, scarcely an instant, and then walked hastily away. I had not stirred, nor taken any note of outward things, when I heard my name uttered, in rather a stern voice, by my father.

Starting up, I turned upon him a crimsoning face.

"Do you know that young man?" he asked, his eye reading my face with an eagerness of gaze I had never experienced before. It seemed as if he was looking right down into my thoughts.

"I do not." My answer was a stammering one.

"Edith, take care! Don't deceive me!" My father had grown calmer than when he first spoke —calmer, at least, externally.

"Why should I deceive you?" I asked, regaining my self-possession, and looking up into his face with a gaze so steady that his eyes turned aside.

"Then you don't know him?" He spoke in evident relief.

"No, sir."

"You observed him yesterday?"

I said "Yes" with what indifference I could assume.

"And again to-day?"

"Yes, sir."

"Evidently," said my father, "he put himself out to attract your attention. There was no occasion for his call here to-day. It was only an excuse. I know him well; and I tell you now, Edith, to beware of him. He's a presuming upstart!"

I did not answer. How could I? But my father seemed to expect me to say something, and stood gazing down upon me. My eyes had fallen to the floor, but I felt that his were on my face, reading it as intently as if he were scanning the pages of a book. He was not satisfied; and no wonder. To such an injunction, no response but a full, out-spoken one, can be satisfactory. If I had smiled indifferently, and spoken in a light, careless way of the young man, as of one about whom I knew nothing and cared less, my father would have accepted the affirmation with a mind partly assured at least. But silence and unconcealed embarrassment left him on a sea of doubt. He would have been a wiser man had he left me without deepening still further the impression he had made; without setting the image of that young man in my memory in a circle of pain, where it would ever after be distinctly visible.

"You understand me, Edith!" His voice was imperative.

What could I say? He was pressing me too closely. My father moved back a step or two, and then stood still. I did not look up, but I knew that he was regarding my face and attitude with an eagle-eyed scrutiny. Slowly, at last, he turned from me, and I was alone. With steps that scarcely left a sound behind them, I went up to my room, shut the door, and locked it. My heart was beating almost wildly. Why should my father act in so strange a way? Who was this young man, that his daring to look towards me should occasion so much disturbance? Aunt Mary knew him. When she said that she must speak a word with him, there was nothing in her voice or manner that could be construed into repulsion or dislike. She had talked with him in a familiar way, as the sound of their voices, which came to my ears, plainly intimated. All these things floated in my thoughts, and were dwelt upon, as I sat dreaming, musing and pondering, in a new and strange state of mind, for a long time. As for the yet unknown person, whose single glance towards me had so greatly disturbed my father, he had become invested with vaguely imagined but imposing attributes. He could be no ordinary young man, that was clear, or my father would have cared nothing for him. I was satisfied of this. His face I had seen twice. I might not have remembered it very distinctly, but for the spur to memory which I had received. Now I recalled and dwelt upon it, until I knew every feature as well as if his miniature had been in my hands. It was a handsome, intelligent, manly face, full of noble feelings. Just the face to make an impression on a woman's heart. It had made already on mine an ineffaceable impression.

"Here is my destiny!" said I at last, as the image gained newer and newer distinctness in my thought. "I have neither stepped aside nor forward to meet it; I have not sought it in restless infatuation. It has met me in the way, and I cannot pass it by if I would!"

It had been my purpose to ask Aunt Mary about the young man, but now I changed this intention. I would wait and let events shape themselves. That we should meet, face to face and at no distant period, I felt certain. Till then, I would be silent to every one.

CHAPTER XI.

MY father's uneasiness could not be concealed. When we met again at dinner-time, and in the evening, I would detect his eyes, if I looked up at him suddenly, fixed upon my countenance with a look of earnest inquiry. His concern obliterated from his mind all perceptive wisdom. If he had reflected for a moment, he must have seen that his conduct was calculated to give the matter an undue importance in my eyes—to turn my thoughts towards the young man instead of away from him.

On the next morning, after breakfast, I went into the parlor again. But not, as on the day before, to linger at the window, waiting for the stranger's appearance, should he call again. I sat down at the piano, with my back to the window, and commenced playing. This would satisfy my father, and assure him, if the young man came, that I would remain in ignorance of the fact. How far was it from his imagination that I played and sang to each visitor who called—I could hear every ring of the bell and every footfall in the passage—in the hope that ears I longed already to penetrate with my voice, would take in the melodies that passed, warbling, full of heart-warmth, from my lips.

Thus I played and sang until the close of my father's office hours. How much I desired to know whether the young man had called. It was several times on my lips to put the question to Aunt Mary. But a dictate of prudence restrained me. I must for the present, at least, keep my own secret beyond the danger of betrayal.

"You look dull this morning," said Aunt Mary. "Are you not staying in the house too much?"

"Perhaps I am," was my reply.

"Put on your things and take a walk, and make some calls."

Just the suggestion that pleased me.

"I think the fresh air of this beautiful day would put new life into my veins." And I went to my room and dressed myself with more than usual carefulness. Was I thus careful for common eyes? No! What then? Did I expect to meet "my destiny"—and was I attiring myself for him? I will not answer "yea" nor "nay." My state of mind was not clear to me. I acted from something like a double consciousness. I was led by an impulse that I neither sought to define nor to control. Yet, all the while, away down in my heart, was a low, delicious thrill— half pain, half pleasure.

It was a calm, sweet, summer day, with the bluest of blue skies bending over the flower-gemmed earth. The air was clear as crystal, and I drank it in like an elixir of life, as I passed through the garden gate, and walked with light steps down the broad pavement, on which lay the still, dense shadows from trees in which the winds slept pulseless. Our house stood a little way from the business portion of the town, in a part where many handsome dwellings had been erected. They stretched along for many squares, each with its little garden in front glowing with flowers, and filling the air with perfume. I had friends in some of these houses, and at almost any other time I would have found more pleasure in calling than in continuing a solitary walk. But, scarcely looking from the right to the left, I kept on, until I reached the less attractive parts of the town, where the noise, and bustle, and rude jar of business stunned the quiet ear.

I was in a strange state of mind; and I knew it. A dreamy, expectant state. Suddenly I was startled by a confused noise in the street behind me—the sound of hoofs and wheels and quick warning voices. I stood still in vague alarm; and as I turned in the direction from which the tumult came, I saw a horse and wagon dashing down towards me. I was near the curb; but, like one in a nightmare, I could not move. Quick falling terror had paralysed me. In a moment more, the frightened animal, who came onwards with widely springing feet, fluttering mane, and distended nostrils, would have struck me with his iron hoofs, when I was seized by strong arms and carried back from the point of danger. Scarcely had I left the spot, when the horse swept by like a fury.

"Thank God, you are safe!"

I did not know the voice. It was disturbed, and full of interest and gratitude, like the voice of one who had saved the life of a beloved object. I was leaning against him heavily, for I had become weak as a child, and could not support myself. Remembering that I was in the street, and seeing a little crowd of persons beginning to gather, one and another of whom were asking whether I was hurt or not, I made an effort to rally myself, and was successful. Disengaging my person from the arm by which I was still supported, I stood up firmly, and turned to look into the face of my rescuer and thank him. But, when I saw his face, I was dumb. Not a word of utterance was on my lips. I could not make a sound. Only with my eyes did I reward him.

The exclamation of Aunt Mary, when I arrived at home, told how much the circumstance had disturbed me.

"What has happened?" she asked, with alarm pictured in her face.

I related the incident of the runaway horse, mentioning that I had been pulled back just in time to save me, but said nothing in regard to the individual to whom I owed my life. My father heard, incidentally, of the circumstance, and hurried home in some alarm, arriving soon after me. My face was still pale, and my nerves disturbed. He made particular inquiries into all the circumstances, and asked who had rescued me. I felt his eyes on my face, as I turned mine partly aside, and answered, truly, that I did not know. And yet I did know my rescuer to be the young man whose presumption in looking towards me had so troubled my father. But who was he? His name and personality were yet unknown to me.

"Did you see his face?" asked my father.

"Only for an instant, as I recovered from the sudden fright, and got away as quickly as possible from the crowd that began to gather around me."

My father was silent for a little while, and, as

I could see, not at ease in his mind. Is it possible, thought I, that he has learned who it was that put forth so timely a saving hand?

"If you should learn who it was," said I, "thank him in my name."

"We, indeed, owe him thanks." My father spoke with some feeling.

The incident coming to the ears of several intimate friends, there were a dozen calls during the day. Some had heard that I was seriously injured; others that I had fainted from alarm; and others some version of the case about as near the truth.

"You had quite an adventure, I hear," said one lady, looking less serious than most of our friends had been in referring to the matter. "A sudden danger, a fright, a fainting fit, and a nice young man to the rescue, just in the nick of time!"

"Oh, no, no!" I answered; "you are wide of the truth. There was no fainting in the case."

"But a nice young man, ha, my pretty lady! That part of the story, at least, is true."

"I was saved by a stranger," said I.

"Are you sure?"

"Very sure." I spoke in a tone of confidence.

The visitor looked at Aunt Mary.

"You know who it was?"

Aunt Mary shook her head.

"Is it possible!"

"Quite so."

"Didn't the doctor tell you?"

"No. I think he is quite as ignorant as we are," said Aunt Mary.

"Not a bit of it. My husband came up a few moments after the incident, and saw the 'noble youth' who had risked his life in the cause of beauty. From him the doctor learned the name of that 'noble youth.' And he has kept it a secret! Well, 'pon my honor!"

"Who was it?" asked Aunt Mary.

"Fairfield & Co.'s handsome clerk. You know him."

"Mr. Holman?"

"Yes."

"Is it possible!"

My aunt looked surprised; but there was no special meaning in her eyes as she turned them upon my face.

"It is singular," she remarked, "that the doctor did not mention his name. He knows him very well."

"He was afraid, I suppose, of this young lady's heart. Gratitude is often the parent of love. Are you very susceptible, my dear?"

"I was thought cold-hearted at school," said I, putting on an air of indifference.

"But had a lover for all that."

"No. I am still heart-free." I tried to speak gaily, but don't think I succeeded.

"Well, well, child," said the visitor, in her light, thoughtless manner, "Cupid has drawn a bow for you now; and the arrow is on its way.' Then turning to Aunt Mary, she added—

"It was a narrow escape, I hear; and you owe the young man a debt of gratitude. His life, they say, was in imminent danger."

A clerk in Fairfield & Co.'s store, named Holman! So much known. After the lady retired, I said to Aunt Mary—

"Then you know this young man, to whom we are all so much indebted."

"Oh, yes; very well," she answered.

My ear was in every tone of her voice; but I could not discover a sign of objection. Many questions came crowding to my lips; but I kept them back, and hid the almost irrepressible interest that was in my heart.

"He's an excellent young man," said Aunt Mary, "and quite a favorite with all who know him."

What music was in the words! I sat silent, but listening intently.

"Handsome, well educated, gentlemanly, and of irreproachable character."

How little did dear Aunt Mary know of the

sweetness that lay in these words as they fell upon my ears. "Handsome, well educated, gentlemanly, and of irreproachable character." They were fixed in my memory, and dwelt upon as testimonials of worth above all gainsaying. I would take Aunt Mary's approval in the face of a denouncing world. How I longed to press inquiry after inquiry; but a prudent forethought made me assume an indifference which I did not feel. My father's attitude towards the young man was a warning to be circumspect.

In the evening, as we sat at the tea-table, Aunt Mary said, addressing my father—

"So it is young Edgar Holman to whom we are so deeply indebted?"

My father looked across the table at Aunt Mary in a cold way, and with a glance of caution in his eyes. I saw it, and the effect upon my aunt. His answer was a simple, indifferently spoken "Yes," and no more was said on the subject.

One might as well attempt to keep water from finding its level, as the heart from obedience to its native impulses. Did my father's strange conduct deaden the impulses of my heart? No—it only quickened them!

In less than a week I met Mr. Holman at the house of one of our friends, where a small company had been invited. I saw him speak to the lady whose guests we were, a few minutes after I came in,

when she brought him to where I was sitting, and
gave us a formal introduction. As he drew a
chair nearly in front of me, and sat down, with
his eyes reading my face as if it were a book, I said
to him—

"Let me, first of all, thank you for my life.
But for the promptness and courage you displayed,
I must have been killed."

My voice trembled, though I tried to speak
calmly, and I was conscious of a deepening color.
His countenance lighted up with a glow of pleasure,
and his eyes looked with more than admiration on
my face.

"I am only too happy," he replied, "in having
been the instrument of rescue. It was a narrow
escape," he added. "If I had been a moment
later, the infuriated horse would have been upon
you. I have shuddered at the thought many times
since."

This was our introduction. For the whole of
that evening, the young man was away from my
side for scarcely a moment. What a charm for
my ears lay in his voice; what a fascination in
his eyes, whenever I could venture to look into
them; what a subduing power in his presence!
Every sentiment he uttered seemed to have in it
deeper meanings than the simple words conveyed,
and my thoughts searched busily all the while
for these meanings. When the hour for sepa-

ration came, he asked to be my escort home.
I knew that my father would call for me in his
carriage, but I could not resist the temptation to
lay my hand upon the arm of Mr. Holman, and
be all alone with him for the first time, and so
accepted his invitation. I hurried on my things,
lest my father should arrive, and passed from the
house with a hand drawn within the arm of Edgar
Holman, my consciousness more like that of a
person in the mazes of a sweet dream than of one
in real life.

"Where is your father?" asked Aunt Mary,
when I met her on entering our house.

"I came away before he arrived," said I.

"How so?" She looked at me narrowly.

"The company was dispersing, and he had not
come, so I accepted an escort. I thought it possible
that he was detained by some patient."

"Who came home with you?"

I tried to speak in a tone of indifference, as I
replied—

"Mr. Holman, my gallant rescuer."

"I'm afraid your father will not be pleased,"
said Aunt Mary, looking at me with a sober
face.

"Why not?"

I believed her, but wished to get at the secret
of my father's too evident dislike of Edgar
Holman.

" He said that he would call for you; and it will displease him when he finds that you went home without waiting for him. He is peculiar, you know."

But this did not satisfy me.

" He doesn't like Mr. Holman," said I.

" How do you know?" My aunt looked at me curiously.

" What is the reason?" I put my question without answering hers.

" 1 am not aware of any dislike towards Mr. Holman, on the part of your father," she replied. " Why have you taken it for granted? Or has our friend made so free as to venture a suggestion of this nature?"

" Oh, no, no!" I answered quickly. " Father was not referred to by him."

I think from the way Aunt Mary looked at me, that my face betrayed more than I wished her to see.

" There is your father, now!" she said, as we heard the door open, and his unusually quick tread in the passage. We were standing in the parlor. He saw us, and came in hastily. His face was angry, as he fixed his eyes on me, and said, with unusual sternness—

" Why did you leave before I came?"

" The company were separating, and I thought you might be detained by some pressing call."

"Didn't I say that I would come for you?" he demanded.

The tone, so angry and imperative beyond anything that I had heard, coufounded me.

"I didn't suppose you would care," I stammered, my eyes filling with tears.

"I do care, then! And now let me say to you, once for all, that I will be your attendant home from evening visits and parties. Do you understand?"

I made no answer. Rebellion was coming into my heart.

"Why don't you speak?"

Still I kept silent. My father's face was growing dark with anger. At this moment Aunt Mary leaned towards him and said something that I did not hear. Whatever it was, it had an immediate influence, for I saw a change in his manner. Without looking towards me, or saying another word, he left the room, and crossing the passage, entered his office and shut the door.

My father had drawn the string too tightly, and snapped the bow. I was a rebel from that hour. Half the night I lay in a kind of semi-conscious elysian dream. I had met my "destiny," face to face; and we had looked away down into each other's eyes, that were only the mirrors of our hearts. All hope, all happiness, all that made life to be desired, were, I felt, included in the love of Edgar Holman. What a strong, deep-flowing passion had suddenly flooded my heart. From a light-thoughted girl, I had become, in a day, as it were, a full-grown, thrillingly-conscious woman.

"My father must not attempt to thwart me here," said I, as I pondered in sober mood, on the next morning, the incidents of the evening before. "I will render him dutiful obedience in all things that a daughter can render as a daughter. But, as a woman, I claim to be the disposer of my own heart. That is free, by God's gift; and free it shall remain! Here, a father's authority does not reach; and I will not acknowledge it."

Bold, strong words for a girl at my age. But I was in earnest. I had been seized upon, as it were, suddenly by a passion that infused itself into every element of my being. Not so much a bewildering, as a deeply-penetrating and all-involving passion. Not agitating and blinding, but strong, clear-seeing, and conclusive. I no more doubted the inspiration of love in the heart of Edgar than I doubted that which had been born in my own. "We were made for each other," said I, in my strange confidence. "And what Heaven ordains is inevitable."

There was a cloud on my father's face when we met on the next morning, but no allusion was made to the evening's disturbing incident. Aunt Mary looked almost as sober as my father. I noticed several times that she was attempting to read my countenance. I made it as a sealed book, however. School-life had taught me lessons of self-control and the art of veiling the face, as well as more intellectual things. I was not yet ready to offer her my confidence. It was far from her thoughts that I had given my heart away ere it had been asked for in any language but heart-language. That I had passed in a few hours from a weak girl to a strong woman. Yet it was so.

CHAPTER XII.

Y father had gone out after tea to make a professional call, and I was dreaming love's young dreams, in an atmosphere of melody which my own fingers were weaving, as I sat at the piano, when a visitor was shown into the parlor. I did not hear the entrance of any one. A slight sound caused me to turn, and there stood Mr. Holman, not more than a pace from me, his face lighted up with an expression that showed him to have been an almost entranced listener to the music I was drawing from my fine-toned instrument.

I felt glad to see him; and the gladness went into my face and told my heart's story.

"Don't stop playing," said he, after I had laid my hand in his, with just a little maiden shyness —felt, not assumed. "I love music—that is, good music."

I turned to the piano and played and sang a

tender love-song. Why did I do this? Of design? Oh no! The song came first to my thoughts, and I gave it to my voice without reflection. If I had meant to tell him what was in my heart, I could not have done it in more fitting words, and I became conscious of this as the last strain died on my lips. Then I felt alarmed lest he should have misunderstood me. Maiden delicacy was wounded at the thought. He did not speak after I had finished. In the silence, I ran my fingers over the keys to a lighter measure, and flung my voice spiritedly into a patriotic song. This he praised warmly; and then turning over the music, selected a nocturne by Chopin, and asked if I could play it. It happened to be one of my favorite pieces. I had practised and enjoyed it so many times that I could give the sentiment a tenderness equal, I had sometimes thought, to that which filled the composer's mind when he brought down the chords and melodies from that inner world to which his ear was opened.

"Do you like that nocturne?" I asked, as I laid the music open before me, looking around into his face as I spoke.

"Yes."

I took my eyes from his, and turned to read the pages that my fingers were to interpret for him. Softly, almost tremulously, I pressed the keys in the tender opening passages, and, as I progressed, entering into the theme, my touches obeyed my feelings and I almost lost myself in what seemed more like an inspiration than a performance. I had never played with such skill before. My listener gave but few words of praise; but I saw that his eyes were humid as I looked up into his face.

"It is my favorite piece," said I.

"And mine." He said no more.

"*Our* favorite piece!" That was spoken in my heart, perhaps in his also.

"How do you like this?" And I selected a few passages from one of Beethoven's Sonatas—passages that a true lover of music can never hear without feeling himself on the threshold of a new world of emotion.

"That must be from Beethoven," he said, as the last note died upon the ear. "How well you interpret him!" he added, as, bending over, he read the composer's name.

Ah, but these few words of praise were sweet! And so he loved music that I loved—music that spoke to a higher soul-sense than existed in common minds—music that stirred the heart in its profounder depths.

Then I tried his appreciation of Mozart and Haydn, and with all the success I desired. Passages that I loved seemed to speak to him as they did to me, for he asked me to repeat them over and over again, each time showing, by his remarks, a taste and comprehension higher than I had found in any one since parting with a school friend, whose intense love of music had helped me to enter beyond the outer court of harmony.

"Do you play?" I asked, in half surprise at finding his ear so critical.

"No," he answered, "but I love music."

I was turning the leaves of a book for another favorite piece, when my father's voice and tread in the hall sent the blood back, coldly, to my heart. The parlor door was pushed open, and he entered. I was sitting at the piano, and Mr. Holman stood bending over my shoulder, looking at the music.

"My father," said I, trying to speak without the betrayal of what I felt; rising from the piano and turning from it as I uttered my father's name.

Mr. Holman smiled in an unembarrassed way, and offering his hand, said with a degree of familiarity that showed him to be no stranger—

"Good evening Doctor—— ! "

My father did not take the offered hand, but said—

"Good evening, Edgar." In the coldest and most unwelcome way was this uttered.

My father sat down on a sofa. Mr. Holman sat down; and I took a chair on the opposite side of the room.

"It has been a pleasant day," remarked Mr. Holman.

My father growled, rather than spoke, an answer, which was as uncivil in language as in manner. I was pained and indignant.

Again our visitor made a remark, and again my father insulted him by a curtness of reply that could not help stinging a sensitive mind.

"Pardon me, sir," said the young man, "if I have intruded." And he arose as he spoke.

I started to my feet, with a face all crimson with mortification and anger. My father arose also, but with a cold, repellent manner—bowing to our visitor's remark, but not answering it in words.

"Good evening Doctor ——!" There was a gentlemanly dignity about Mr. Holman, as he returned the bow, that was in striking contrast with my father's conduct and aspect. Then he looked towards me; and our eyes met. I let him see more in mine than I would have dared to do under any other circumstances; and I read in his eyes enough to satisfy my heart.

"Please remember," said my father imperatively, as soon as Mr. Holman had retired, "that if that fellow calls here again, you are not to see him."

I did not answer. The term "fellow," as applied to Edgar Holman, seemed such an outrage that I felt too indignant to trust my lips in a response.

"Did you hear me?" demanded my father.

"It is not to be presumed that he will call again," said I, speaking with forced calmness, "after the treatment he has just received. Rather a strange return, it strikes me, for a life risked to save your child's life!"

My father was a little staggered at this, and I saw it. He had forgotten, I will believe, in his sudden displeasure at seeing Edgar, the great obligation we all owed him.

"I have my reasons, Edith, for not wishing you to encourage that young man's visits." He spoke less coldly.

"If you will state the reasons, father," said I, "you may help me to the means of obedience."

"What do you mean?" He turned upon me in a quick, stern way.

"Father," I spoke calmly, for I was growing more and more self-possessed every moment, "you lay upon me a necessity for saying what I would rather a thousand times leave unsaid."

The sternness of his face did not relax. I remained silent, hoping that he would see his own false position, and the danger of driving me into open antagonism. But it never seemed to enter his mind that I was anything but a child, whose will must be subordinate to his will.

"Speak!" he exclaimed, at last.

I stood, still silent, for a little while, and then said, in a low, but quiet, distinct, and meaning voice,

"I am a woman."

He did not, at first, comprehend what I wished him to see.

"Ah, indeed!" He spoke just a trifle sarcastically. This quickened my pulses.

"Yes, sir, a woman; and in all matters where the heart is concerned, answerable alone to God! Forgive me for saying this, but you press me too hard."

The blood that had been burning in my father's face left it instantly, and he looked so pale that I became alarmed.

"Oh, sir," I said, in a distressed voice, as I came forward and caught one of his hands in mine, "I did not mean to hurt or offend you. Don't look so, father! You frighten me! Dear father!" and I laid my face upon him and lost myself in tears and sobs.

"Ungrateful child!" He pushed me resolutely away, while I clung to him eagerly.

"I never thought to hear such words from child of mine!

> "Ingratitude! thou marble-hearted fiend,
> More hideous, when thou show'st thee in a child,
> Than the Sea Monster."

And he pushed me firmly still away.

But my father overacted his part in giving this quotation from Shakspeare. His tone was theatric enough to jar upon my finely adjusted ear. It seemed to me like trifling. And so I yielded to the repulsive hand that was against me, and let it bear me back as far as it would. The color was coming into his face as I looked up into it again; but I think mine must have been white as marble, for something in it appeared to startle him.

"Go to your room," he said, with less unkindness of tone. "We will talk of this another time."

But I did not stir.

"Go, my child." His voice was gentler.

"Not yet, father," I said. "Better talk now, while in the way of this subject. It can do no good to wait." And I sat down.

My father looked perplexed. He saw that in me which he had never seen before. I had said to him that I was a woman, and the meaning of my words was beginning to dawn upon his mind. He knit his brows and bent his eyes, with recovering sternness, upon me. But I was not intimidated. I felt that a struggle for womanly freedom had been forced upon me, and that I must conquer.

"It was not like you, father, to treat any one as you treated that young man to-night," said I, coming to the issue with a kind of desperate courage. "If there is anything wrong about him, let me know what it is. If his life or principles are bad or if there be any facts in regard to him that should be thrown up as a barrier to acquaintanceship, speak of them to me father. They shall not be disregarded."

"Is not my word of disapproval enough?" he asked. "If I say to my daughter, 'Do not receive a certain visitor,' is not that sufficient?"

"It might be under some circumstances," I replied, firmly. "It is not in this."

"Blind, self-willed girl!" He lost himself in passion again. I sat without replying, my thoughts growing clearer and clearer, and my feelings calmer.

"I am older than you are." My father, when he spoke again, tried to address my reason and my pride. "I have seen more of the world. I understand character better. My judgment is more matured. It is from this superior state that I now speak to you, and warn you, as you value your best interest in life, to beware of this young man. Keep yourself free from all entanglements. You are young, and can make, in time, the best alliance our city has to offer, if you will. Look up, not down. What is this Holman but a clerk? A mere adventurer from the East! Don't stoop to him, when you may win the best and noblest!

Wait—wait. Hold yourself a little in reserve until you can meet the best men of our city—men who dwarf, by comparison, this little presuming upstart into insignificance."

If my father had sought to create an interest in my mind favorable to Mr. Holman, he could not have taken a more effectual way. How blind he was! He knew human nature better than this. But his impatience threw all right perception into obscurity; and so, while he endeavored to destroy my first impressions, he only made them stronger.

We parted for the night without coming to a mutual good understanding. He tried to extort a promise that I would repulse Edgar Holman if he made any advances towards me; but I answered that gratitude alone would require that I should always treat him with considerate kindness. He had saved my life. Against this my father had no conclusive reasons to urge, because there was nothing to be said against the spotless character of the man who had come so suddenly between him and worldly ambition.

CHAPTER XIII.

ROM that time, my father's manner towards me was different. A night of sober thought convinced him, without doubt, that I possessed a quality and a development of will that must be treated in a way altogether different from that in which he had begun to meet the impediment so unexpectedly thrown in his path. When I met him on the next morning, he was serious but kind in his manner; and with the kindness of tone used in addressing me, I now and then detected a new feeling, which seemed more like respect for something he had discovered in me than aught else to which I could compare it.

The conclusion in my own mind was natural. I had shown myself too strong for him. No feeling of triumph accompanied this; but it gave me a certain confidence in myself. As my father had assumed a new character, so to speak, in order more surely to gain his ultimate purposes in regard to me—which purposes began to dawn in my thoughts—I put on an exterior designed to mislead him. I do not think, however, that either was much deceived by the other.

I did not tell Aunt Mary about my father's treatment of Mr. Holman, nor allude to the painful interview that followed. It was at first my intention to do so, and to take her entirely into my confidence. But on reflection, I changed my mind. For the present, at least, I would keep my own counsel. I was satisfied, from her manner, that she was not even aware that my father had seen Mr. Holman in the parlor. Her pleasant banter in regard to my visitor gave me an opportunity to ask some questions about him, in a casual way, as though I had but little interest in her replies. I found that he was something of a favorite with Aunt Mary; and that she regarded him as a very superior young man. Her opinion of any one, I would take against the world, so that disposed entirely of my father's objections.

Mr. Holman did not call again. This was as I had expected. After my father's uncivil treatment, self-respect must keep him away. I soon became aware that all my movements were closely observed by my father. If I went out, he, somehow or other, managed to cross my way in the street—sometimes twice or thrice. If I paid an evening visit, he was sure to come for me at an early hour. If I attended a party, he was there long before the time arrived for the company to disperse. Whenever it happened that Mr. Holman was present, and ventured to come near me, which he always did, my father's manner exhibited disturbance, and he would use various little arts to interrupt our intercouse, or procure a separation of one from the other. This became so apparent that neither of us could help noticing it or being annoyed thereby. Is it remarkable that this studied effort to keep us apart should have the effect to draw us more closely together, and precipitate the result he so dreaded?

One evening I met Mr. Holman at an entertainment given by Mrs. Fairfield, the wife of a member of the mercantile house in which he was a clerk. It was a large company, and some of our best people, as they are called, were there. As usual, greatly to the annoyance of my father, who was present, Edgar soon found his way to my side; and when the dancing commenced, we took the floor as partners. Two or three times, as we stood in the pauses of the dance, I met my father's eyes bent almost sternly upon me. At the close of the set, my partner led me to a sofa, and stood before me, talking, when my father came up with a gentleman, and presented him to me as a Mr

Congreve. Edgar retired to another part of the room. •

"May I claim your hand for the next cotillion?" asked the gentleman, bowing very low, and with what struck me as an excess of formality.

. I could not say that I was already engaged, and even if I had been, to Edgar, I would not have ventured to decline, under the circumstances. Until the next set took the floor, Mr. Congreve held me in conversation, and I had a good opportunity to observe him. I was nineteen; he past thirty. So much for the difference in our ages. I did not like his face. It was strongly marked, and gave evidence of mental vigor, but not of refinement or taste. His nose was large and slightly aquiline; his eyes prominent; his lips full; his complexion dark. He was rather above than below the middle stature.

I saw many curious eyes upon us as we stood up and took a position on the floor; and from the expression in some of these eyes, I understood that my partner was a man of mark for something distinguishing. Large wealth, I afterwards learned this to be. He made quite an elegant appearance, as he threaded the mazy figures, and I might have been proud of my partner if his company had not, at the time, been almost an intrusion.

"You dance charmingly," he said, as the music ceased, and we passed to the side of the room; "and before somebody else snatches you away from me, I must secure your hand for another set."

I could do no less than consent. My father now joined us, and looked happy as Mr. Congreve complimented me. I danced with him again; and then he drew me away from the parlors to the conservatory, which had been lighted up for the occasion, and held me there, in conversation about rare plants, with which he seemed familiar, for nearly an hour. Three or four times Edgar passed near us; and I saw, by the expression of his face, that he was annoyed, and, perhaps, a little disturbed in mind. I tried to throw him assuring glances.

"I must follow up this acquaintance," said Mr. Congreve, speaking both to me and to my father, as we stood together in the thinning parlors, at a late hour.

My father bowed; but I made no response. The intimation was far from being agreeable. As we rode home, my father spoke warmly of Mr. Congreve. He was a man of wealth and high position, he said, who had come to our city from the South a year before, to connect himself with some enterprises of an extensive character. I listened, but did not answer. His wealth and position, however attractive to my father, had no charms for me. As a man, he had not impressed me favorably.

Indisposition had prevented Aunt Mary from attending this party of the season; a circumstance that we both regretted. I went to her room, on my return home, and found her awake. She had many questions to ask, as to who were there, and how I had enjoyed the evening. I mentioned my introduction to Mr. Congreve, and his monopoly of my company. She did not seem altogether pleased.

"Who is he, aunt? Tell me!" I spoke with some earnestness.

"I cannot say that I know much about him," she replied. "He has not resided here for a very long time."

"Father says he is very rich."

"Money isn't everything." Aunt Mary said this partly to herself.

"What do you think of him?" I wanted to get her impression of the man.

"He has not been a favorite of mine," was her reserved answer.

"He is going to call here," said I.

"How do you know?" Aunt Mary spoke with sudden interest.

"He said that he meant to follow up the acquaintance. I suppose that means what I intimate."

"Perhaps it does." A faint sigh closed the remark.

"I don't like him," said I.

Aunt Mary looked at me curiously.

"And I don't wish him to come here," I added.

"It may only have been a compliment," said Aunt Mary. "Men of his stamp are often profuse in words."

"He has plenty of them. I wished him dumb more than a dozen times to-night. He really persecuted me with his compliments and attentions."

"Don't think any more about them, dear." Aunt Mary looked a little worried, I thought.

"You don't like him?" said I, determined to get her impression of Mr. Congreve.

"Not much," she replied. "He isn't the kind of man to win my admiration."

"Nor mine either," I responded. "So, he might as well save himself the trouble of following up the acquaintance."

I kissed Aunt Mary, and said good night. I was in too much excitement of mind to sleep for an hour or two after retiring. There was trouble in my way; I saw that clearly. If Mr. Congreve should prove to be really in earnest in his admiration, and attempt any advances beyond the formalities of ordinary acquaintanceship, I should have to hold him off, at the risk of offending my father.

In the morning my father asked me how I had enjoyed the party, and ere I could reply said, smiling,

"But I had eyes, and could see for myself. She was quite the belle." And he looked across the table at Aunt Mary.

My heart did not flutter nor my face crimson at this compliment; I felt too sober for that.

" Dissipation is not good for you." My father looked at me more narrowly. " You danced too often last night."

" Perhaps I did." I spoke listlessly.

My father then gave Aunt Mary some account of the entertainment, and of the people who were there. As I expected, he said more about Mr. Congreve than any one else, and sought to make a good impression in regard to him. I kept silent, and so did Aunt Mary. He was a little annoyed at this, I could see, but repressed his feelings.

Almost to my consternation, Mr. Congreve made me a call this very morning. I could do no less than treat him courteously; but he found me, at home, something different, I imagine, from what he found me in company on the night before.

" Are you fond of music ? " he asked, as we sat conversing. My suggestive piano stood open in the room.

I replied in the affirmative.

"So am I, passionately," he said. "Won't you favor me?" and he made a motion to lead me to the instrument. I arose and crossed to where it stood, without suffering him to touch my hand.

"What kind of music do you like?" I inquired, as I sat down, and laid a book open on the desk.

"Oh, anything that can be called music," he replied.

I tried him in a piece designed to reach only a cultivated ear, and understood from his undiscriminating praise that it merely gave to his sense of hearing a confusion of musical sounds. A march reached him more intelligibly, so did an airy waltz. The Nocturne by Chopin received the equivocal praise contained in the words "very fine."

"You play charmingly," he said, as I left the piano. "Charmingly!" he added. "I never heard better playing in my life, and I have listened to some admirable performers, both at home and abroad."

I acknowledged the compliment as gracefully as possible. He then referred to some musical entertainments which he had enjoyed, a few years before, in London and Paris, and mentioned certain celebrities, in whom I felt interested.

My replies led him on to speak of other things connected with his tour in Europe, and, as he had been quite an intelligent observer, he soon had my absorbed attention. He must be a dull man indeed, who has spent any time in Paris, London, Rome, Florence, and Naples, and yet is not able to interest the thought of a young and ardent girl, who has dreamed over their fascinations in books. But Mr. Congreve was far from being a dull man. He was, on the contrary, intelligent, appreciative, and a lover of art. He had travelled with open eyes, and brought home a well stored memory.

He saw that I was interested in his reminiscences and descriptions, and entertained me for an hour with pictures of Italian life, scenery, and art. When he took his departure, my impression of the man was changed. I could not but feel respect for his intelligence, and a certain deference towards him as one who had seen the world at many points, and enjoyed rare advantages.

I mentioned the call to my father, and saw that it gave him great pleasure. It would have been more in accordance with my feelings to have said nothing to him on the subject; but I had my reasons for alluding to the visit.

"He is really an intelligent man," said I to Aunt Mary, in speaking to her of Mr. Congreve. "He travelled in Europe with open eyes, and describes what he saw in a very interesting manner."

"He is a man possessed of considerable information," replied my aunt; "but——"

She paused, as if questioning with herself the propriety of saying what was in her thoughts.

"But what, Aunt Mary?" I said, seeing that she hesitated.

"Two things go to make up the character of a true man," she remarked.

"What are they?"

"The head and the heart; or the intellect and the moral qualities."

"That I understand clearly."

"The head is well enough in the case of Mr. Congreve," said Aunt Mary; "but I am not so well satisfied about the heart."

"I know one thing," said I; "there is about him, for me, a sphere of repulsion. I felt all the while as if something were pushing me away from him. Was it not singular, to say the least of it?"

"It is a fact not lightly to be regarded," was Aunt Mary's reply. "When two persons meet for the first time, this feeling of repulsion on the part of one or the other often occurs, and is not without significance."

"What does it signify?" I saw that Aunt Mary was not speaking at random—indeed, she never does that—but had a meaning that involved something beyond what my girlish thoughts had ever reached.

"It may signify perception of quality," said Aunt Mary.

"I am not sure that I understand you," was my reply.

"You can understand that the mind has a quality. That it is good or bad -true or false?"

"Oh, yes." For that was clear enough.

"When two persons meet, and the thought of each turns to the other, we may say, without figure of speech, that their minds meet." Aunt Mary spoke with deliberation, so that I might get the meaning of her words. "Can you see that this is really so?"

"If the mind is a substantial thing, as I have often heard you say, substantial because formed out of spiritual substance, as the body is formed out of material substance, then, in the presence which thought gives, there must be an actual meeting of two minds," I said in reply.

"I see that you comprehend me." Aunt Mary spoke with satisfaction in her tones, and then added: "In this meeting, is it not fair to conclude, that if the quality of one mind be good, and that of the other evil, the quality will be perceived, and a sense of repulsion be inevitable, in one case or the other. Can it be otherwise?"

I caught at the suggestion eagerly. It was novel to my mind, but self-evidently true.

"Does the repulsion of which you speak," I asked, "always indicate evil quality?"

"I think," she replied, "that would be assuming

too much. In nature, electrical attractions and repulsions do not indicate evil quality, but opposite conditions. So it may be as to minds."

"Then," said I, "the inference follows that an instinctive dislike, or repulsion, felt towards any one at first, may be taken as a warning that some condition or quality exists that would for ever prevent an intimate and harmonious association; and that any attempt to act in the face of this warning is a blind folly, opening the way to misery."

"I do not know that you state the case too strongly," remarked Aunt Mary, thoughtfully; "in my view it is safer to obey these suggestive instincts than to disregard them."

"Thank you, dear aunt," said I, "for the light you have thrown into my mind. I just wanted these few rays to guide me in the right path."

Aunt Mary looked at me curiously. But I did not take her yet into my confidence.

CHAPTER XIV.

DID not feel at ease in my mind touching Mr. Congreve. If my heart had not already become interested, and in a direction displeasing to my father, his attentions at the party, and call upon me at so early a period afterwards, would only have stirred a little maiden vanity. Now, the fear lest he might be in earnest troubled me.

I was not long in doubt. He called again in a day or two, and, at this second visit, asked me to ride out with him on the next afternoon. I tried to excuse myself; but in a playful manner, that only concealed an earnest purpose, he pressed me to give consent.

"If my father does not object," I said, at last.

Now, I would rather have said anything else; but in my perplexity, this came forth unwillingly.

"I will answer for your father," replied my visitor in a confident way that amazed me.

"Mr. Congreve has asked me to ride out with him," said I to my father, on meeting him.

"Has he?" I saw his face brighten.

"Yes, on to-morrow afternoon."

"You accepted the attention, of course?"

I shook my head.

"What!" His surprise and disappointment were too apparent.

"Without your approval, sir, I would not think it right to accept such an invitation."

"Did you say so to Mr. Congreve?" he asked.

"I said, if you did not object."

"Oh!" His face brightened again. "I thought you could hardly have been so rude as to decline such a flattering attention from a man like Mr. Congreve."

I turned away to hide my crimsoning face. "A man like Mr. Congreve!" I shut my teeth as I repeated the words in suppressed indignation. The repulsion about which I had spoken to Aunt Mary was felt as strongly as ever at this second visit from Mr. Congreve; and the thought of sitting alone with him in a carriage for two or three hours was exceedingly unpleasant. I had, in addition, a secret fear lest we should be seen riding out together by Mr. Holman; and that he would take more for granted than truth could warrant.

When Mr. Congreve called with his handsome

carriage and splendid pair of horses, I was ready to accompany him. The drive was amid some of the finest scenery in the neighborhood, and my companion interested me in local traditions connected with pioneer settlers; in showing fine points in the landscape; in comparing our scenery with that of countries which he had visited; and in other ways, varied by the suggestions of our ride. It was near the hour of sunset when we drove down towards the city, which lay stretching along and back from the broad river that swept by in a never-ceasing current.

"You have heard of Italian skies?" said Mr. Congreve, as he drew upon the reins until the horses stood still at a turn in the road, from which the whole western horizon was visible. At the zenith, the sky was of a deep blue, with here and there a gauzy scarf of white vapor lying motionless against the pure azure. As the eye descended westward, the number of these white, fleecy masses increased, and between them you saw the sky taking on a pale, transparent green. Lower down, cloud and sky were purpling in warmer rays. Then came a mountain range of white clouds, with dusky gorge and dim valley receding far into its bosom, and every snowy peak crowned with a diadem of golden rays. Below this, was a lake of soft azure and green, its surface as smooth as glass, and below this, a molten sea of fiery sunbeams, yellow and red and purple, that gleamed like molten gems and gold. The scene was one of gorgeous beauty. A sunset to be remembered.

"You have heard of Italian skies?" repeated Mr. Congreve, after I had looked for some time in silence upon the entrancing scene.

"They cannot be more beautiful than that," said I, lifting my finger towards the west.

"Italy never saw anything more glorious," he replied. And then he described for me, as we sat there, with our eyes upon the changing scene, and the horses at rest, a sunset witnessed among the Apennines.

"More beautiful than this" said I, when he ceased speaking, "because the mind gives it a charm not drawn from nature—the charm of association. A sunset viewed from an Ohio bluff, and one from a peak amid the Apennines, must affect the soul differently."

We discussed this point as we rode homewards, he, by a slightly urged difference of opinion, spurring my mind into excitement. I had grown animated, and was combating some playful remark he had made, when—we had entered the city, and were driving down one of the principal streets—my eyes encountered the face of Mr. Holman, and I became silent. I knew that upon my face was a glow of pleasant feeling. What would be the effect on his mind? That was the instant question in my thoughts. Mr. Congreve had almost monopolized me on the night of the party, since which Edgar and I had not met; and now, I was riding with Mr. Congreve, and in animated conversation with him.

For the rest of the drive home I was silent. My companion could not, of course, help noticing the change. The reason was hardly suspected. He tried to interest me by a change of subject, but failed altogether.

My father was standing at the garden gate as we drove up.

"I have returned her safely, Doctor," said Mr. Congreve, as he sprang from his seat and assisted me to alight.

"I hope you have enjoyed the ride," remarked my father.

"I can speak for myself—how is it with you, Miss Edith?" And Mr. Congreve looked with a smiling face into mine.

"I was much gratified." What less could I have said? Then, bowing, I ran along the walk, and disappeared in the house. Full ten minutes must have elapsed before I heard the carriage drive away. Why had Mr. Congreve lingered so long in conversation with my father? The fact disturbed me. I did not imagine for a moment that he had, on so brief an acquaintance, made any serious advances. But I was mistaken.

At tea-time my father was in unusually good spirits. He asked me many questions about our ride, and tried to draw me on to speak of it; but I was sober and had little to say.

"I have a compliment for you," said my father, as he sat with his pleased eyes on my face.

"Who from?" I asked.

"Can't you guess?"

I shook my head.

"From Mr. Congreve."

My father looked at me narrowly. I showed no signs of pleasure.

"Would you like to know what he said?" My father's voice was a little shaded. He was disappointed at my apparent indifference.

"Not particularly," I answered.

"Then you shan't know it!" He was piqued.

"So much saved to my vanity," said I, coldly.

"She's dying to hear, of course," remarked Aunt Mary, who put in this mollifying sentence. She saw that my father was annoyed.

"Don't believe a word of it," I said, quickly. "Mr. Congreve's opinion is of no consequence to me. I don't like him!"

My father's brows closed suddenly, and he showed unmistakable signs of discomfiture.

"He's rich, polished, and intelligent; no one

can gainsay that;" I thought it well to speak out then and there; "but he is not a man after my fancy, and it is the last time, I trust, he will ever ask me to ride with him."

I hardly know what possessed me to speak so boldly; a consciousness of being in imminent danger, perhaps.

"A girl's fancies are the embodiment of all wise appreciation of character, of course!" My father spoke with a curl of his expressive lip.

"Say a woman's perception, father," I replied, calmly, "and you may be near the truth." I let my voice dwell upon the word *woman*, and looked at him with a meaning expression on my face. I wished him to remember a previous conversation which he had forced upon me.

He was about to answer, and with some vehemence, I inferred from the sudden play of his features; but he checked himself, became silent, and did not speak again during the meal. He had remembered that conversation.

CHAPTER XV.

NE afternoon, very soon after that drive with Mr. Congreve, as I was on my way home from a visit to a friend, I met Edgar Holman. It was the first time I had been face to face with him since the night of the party at Mrs. Fairfield's. His countenance did not light up with the usual glow of pleasure that I had heretofore observed in it; and he seemed a little shy and embarrassed. Taking the reason for granted, I laid my hand in his, and let my eyes rest steadily in his eyes. He read their language, and was satisfied.

We stood and talked for a little while, and then parted; not from any sense of repulsion, such as I experienced when in company with Mr. Congreve. On the contrary, the sphere of attraction was as strong in the case of Mr. Holman as the sphere of repulsion was in the case of Mr. Congreve. I had gone a short distance, after parting with Edgar, when I heard his quick steps behind me. Returning to my side, he said, with a little tremor in his voice,

"Are you in a hurry to get home, Miss Edith?"

I replied in the negative.

"Because, if you are not, I thought I would propose a short walk."

Nothing could have been more agreeable at the time. So we turned from the main street, down to a retired part of the city, where the dwellings stood far apart, and rows of well grown trees threw a shade on the sidewalks. Very little was said by either until we were quite beyond the reach of common observation; in fact, almost away from the settled portions of the town. Then taking my hand, in an impulsive way, after a silence of some minutes, Mr. Holman said, hurriedly,

"Pardon me, if I am going too far; but I feel that I must speak now."

He stopped, while I was holding my breath for other words.

"Shall I go on?" he asked. I did not withdraw the hand he had taken; but accorded that much of assent.

"You are not offended?"

"Oh, no!" The words leaped impulsively to expression.

Still, he was not satisfied. He wanted something more assuring.

"You are very dear to me, Edith!" With what a delicious thrill did the sentence go through my heart! And yet, my hand lay in his—passively? I cannot say yea to that.

"My father's approval will never, I fear, be obtained," said I, as soon as I could trust myself to speak.

"And if he says nay, what then?" He looked into my face with tender earnestness.

"We must wait patiently and hopefully for a time."

"And lovingly, Edith," he added. Then, after a little while, he said, "I would not have spoken with such unseemly haste, if I had not been in fear of losing what to me is so precious. Nor would I have taken an opportunity like this, if your father had not deprived me, by his repulsive conduct, of one that would have seemed more honorable. Against anything clandestine, my feelings revolt; and I am hurt at the necessity which compels me to take an apparently unfair advantage of your father. If you do not object, I will, in the face of all unpleasant consequences, call upon him, and claim your hand."

I did not know what answer I should make to this.

"Time will be our instructors," said I, after

pondering the matter. "For the present it were better, I think, to keep this secret locked within our own hearts."

"If you think best, I have not a word to say," he replied.

We had turned, and were now walking homewards. I wanted to speak of Mr. Congreve. I knew that he had seen us riding out together, and I wished him to understand that the man was wholly repulsive. Yet a feeling of maiden delicacy kept me from uttering his name. While the thought of him was yet in my mind, I heard the sound of wheels in advance, and lifting my eyes, I saw him driving towards us in his elegant carriage. As he approached, I raised my hand, and drew it within the arm of my companion, thus acknowledging the existence of something more than acquaintanceship. I saw a disturbed look on his face, as he bowed low, in passing.

I could have done nothing more assuring to Edgar. The plainest spoken words would not have conveyed so clearly my rejection of Mr. Congreve, and acceptance of him.

We parted while yet at some distance from home, and without encountering my father, who, as a physician of good practice, was moving about in all directions. I had been in dread of meeting him nearly all the time.

For a little season, I was happy beyond the

reach of outward things. Edgar and I were born for each other. I felt as much assured of this as of my existence. From the first, even as strangers, we drew mutually together; and at each meeting, the attraction had grown stronger. And now, pledges were exchanged. The brief season of doubt was over; and the assurance of oral language confirmed the significance of look, tone, and expression.

Many circumstances conspired to prevent our meeting again for nearly two weeks. Two or three times during this period Mr. Congreve called to see me, and twice invited me to ride out with him. A fortunate headache gave me a good excuse for declining on both occasions. I treated him with as much coldness as I dared to assume towards a visitor; but he was not, as far as I could see, in the least repelled thereby.

My next meeting with Mr. Holman was in a company at the house of a friend. Mr. Congreve was present; so were my father and Aunt Mary. The rooms were well filled, which gave Edgar and me an opportunity to speak familiarly to one another without attracting observation. He came in a little later than I did, but sought me out immediately. Mr. Congreve arrived soon after.

"Remember," said Edgar, as he noticed Mr. Congreve crossing the room towards us "that,

when the dancing begins, you are engaged to me
for the first set."

"And for the second and third, also, if you
will," was my answer.

Mr. Congreve bowed with impressive formality
as he came up, and I returned his greeting in a
friendly way. He did not notice Edgar in even
a cold nod, but began talking with me as freely as
if we two were alone, referring to his disappointment in not having had the pleasure of my company in a drive two or three days before.

"You would have seen," he said, "a sunset of
even more gorgeous beauty than the one we both
enjoyed so much two or three weeks ago. It far
outrivalled anything that I witnessed in the land
so famed for its glorious skies."

I did not express regret at having missed the
splendid sight, but merely referred to the beautiful sky we had gazed upon as one long to be remembered.

"The point from which we saw it gave the
scene a grander beauty," replied Mr. Congreve.
'Nothing intruded to cut the horizon, and diminish the impression of vastness. I must take you
there again, when the atmosphere is favorable."

But I guarded my reply so as not to express
any desire to accept his proffered courtesy. Gradually, and I thought from design, Mr. Congreve's
person became intruded between me and Edgar

Holman, so that the latter was forced to recede to a greater distance. My father coming up, completely separated us. I felt provoked at what seemed contemptuous treatment of Edgar on the part of Mr. Congreve; and resented it with some coldness of manner.

Music was now introduced, preparatory to dancing. Mr. Congreve immediately claimed my hand for the first set.

I thanked him, but answered that I was already engaged; and Edgar, coming forward at the moment, said—

"I believe you are to be my partner."

I arose and accepted his offered arm. Mr. Congreve looked disappointed, and my father frowned. But I was too happy to be at my lover's side to care very greatly for the disappointment or displeasure of any one.

"For the next set also, remember," said Edgar, as he conducted me to a seat after the dancing was over. Mr. Congreve came to my side again, and Edgar moved away.

"Our young friend was too quick for me," remarked the former, in a pleasant, nonchalant way. "But I will steal a march on every one else. Your hand is free for the next set?"

"No," I answered, smiling, so that I might not seem as cold as I felt.

"I'm disappointed." And tone and look were

in confirmation of his words. "I claim you, then, for the next."

I had said to Edgar that I would dance with him in the second and third sets as well as in the first; but a moment of hurried thought made me conclude, on my father's account, to accept Mr. Congreve for the third set. I could explain to Edgar when we danced together for the second time. So I replied:

"I shall be happy to dance with you then, Mr Congreve."

He looked more pleased than was agreeable to me. I was not vain enough to be flattered by the impression it was clear I had made upon him.

I informed Edgar, in a few words, while we danced for the second time, that I had promised to accept Mr. Congreve as a partner. I saw a slight change on his countenance; but I said that it was on my father's account, and that a certain measure of prudence must be exercised. He assented, but not cheerfully.

"After the third set I will dance no more this evening," said I.

And I did not go on the floor again, though solicited by Mr. Congreve and others. Edgar made his way to where I sat, but the rich Mr. Congreve did not hide his contempt for the poor merchant's clerk, whose unobtrusive, gentlemanly reserve of manner gave the other an opportunity to push him aside and monopolize my company.

Many times during that evening, in looking towards Aunt Mary, I saw her eyes upon me, and noted something unusual in their expression. I also noticed that my father observed me closely, and with much of doubt and question in his manner.

My secret was already burdening me heavily. It was against my nature to act in a hidden or clandestine way, and I resolved to take Aunt Mary into my confidence, and get her clear head and more solid judgment to act with and for me. So on returning home I went to her room instead of to my own, and there told her everything. She sat a long time after I had ceased speaking, before she replied. Her first words were:

"I'm afraid, dear, there is trouble before you."

"I have not questioned that from the beginning," I answered. "But do we not always find less trouble in doing right than in doing wrong?"

"Without doubt," she replied.

"Mr. Congreve is pressing his attentions on me, with, evidently, the full approval of my father. He is wealthy; a man of good social standing; some culture; and more than ordinary intelligence. But he is so repulsive to me that his presence always produces a sense of stricture here," and I laid my hand against my bosom. "The very thought of becoming his wife produces a feeling like suffocation. I could hate much easier than I could love him! Would it be right for me, then, under any pressure of circumstances, to marry him?"

Aunt Mary said "No," in a clear, steady voice.

"On the other hand," I continued, "from the moment I saw Mr. Holman, I felt a motion in my heart away down below the region of any prior consciousness. I was drawn towards him with an unaccountable attraction, which I could no more resist than a leaf can resist the pressure of a steadily moving current. I did not, with an eager, girlish caprice, yield to this impression; and I would not, perhaps, even now have been aware of its true power if my father had not attempted to make me act in opposition. That proved it to be no evanescent influence. The effort on his part to push us asunder only caused the invisible bond by which we had become united to draw heavily upon both of our hearts, and make us deeply conscious of its existence as a real thing. When, therefore, under the fear of losing me, Edgar was impelled to speak of 'what he felt, was I wrong in responding according to the truth?"

To this Aunt Mary did not reply. I waited for some time, and then said:

"Should a woman marry where she does not love?"

Her "No" was unhesitating and emphatic.

"That settles the question in regard to Mr. Congreve, should he really show himself to be in earnest," said I.

"His wealth and position should not come into the estimate?"

"No, no. It is the man as to character, quality, and disposition. As to fitness and congeniality. These alone are to be considered, my child." Aunt Mary spoke with a sudden earnestness. "No mere social condition can give happiness in marriage. Love, in the humblest position, is blessed; but the highest, without love, is a weariness and pain."

"I love Edgar Holman with all my heart," said I, laying my face down upon Aunt Mary's bosom.

"It may be so, my child." Her hand passed caressingly over my brow and temples. "But these sudden impressions are not always permanent. There may be something in this of mere impulse. It may not be grounded in any soul-perception."

"It is, dear aunt, it is!" I answered with ardor. "You know that I was never what is called a susceptible girl. That I was not fond of young gentlemen's society. That beaux were always more disagreeable than pleasant. But from the instant my eyes looked into Edgar's face my heart moved towards him. I cannot help myself if I would. There is an impulse pushing me onwards, that it would be vain to resist. Yes, Aunt Mary, I love Edgar Holman, and for good or evil, my destiny is bound up with his. And now, what is the best thing to do?"

Aunt Mary was silent again.

"Ought I, as things are, to encourage the attentions of Mr. Congreve?"

"I think not," said my aunt.

"Will it not be best for my father to know exactly how it stands with Edgar and me?"

"Undoubtedly."

"Who shall inform him?" I asked.

Aunt Mary reflected for a little while, and then said:

"It will place Edgar in a better position if a communication of the fact first come from him. The matter has gone too far already, as concealed from your father, and the longer it goes the stronger will be his ground of objection."

I was fully in agreement with this, and with so much settled as to the future, left Aunt Mary and went to my own room.

CHAPTER XVI.

N the next day I sent a note to Edgar, asking him to meet me, at a certain hour, in the retired part of the town that was dear to me in memory for the happiness I had there experienced. I related to him, when we met, a part of my conversation with Aunt Mary, and mentioned the advice she had given. He was ready to act upon it, and did so within twenty-four hours. I was not altogether unprepared for the result. My father insulted him in the grossest manner, and forbade any attempt to see me; utterly rejecting his suit at the same time, and telling him that it was hopeless. This he communicated to me by letter, closing with the sentence:

"And what now, dear Edith?"

I answered, telling him that I would be true to him till death, and counselling patience and hope.

Two or three days passed without my father

approaching me on the subject, but I could see that his mind was strongly exercised.

I was coming down stairs, late in the afternoon of the third day since the rejection of Edgar's suit, dressed to go out. It was to keep an appointment with my lover. I had seen him on the day before, and we were to meet again according to agreement. It was full two hours before my father's usual return home. His office hours were from three to four o'clock; after that he was frequently away among his patients until nearly seven. To my surprise, the front door opened and he came in, in something of a hurried manner. Seeing me dressed for the street, he said, a little imperatively—

" Where are you going, Edith ? "

My face commenced burning, and I answered, with a confusion of spirit that I could not overcome—

" To take a walk, sir."

" Come into the parlor. I would like to say a word to you."

I followed him.

" Sit down," he said.

I sat down, and he drew a chair nearly in front of me. He was considerably disturbed in mind.

" You were out at this time yesterday ! " He spoke affirmatively.

"I was." My answer was given without hesitation.

"Where?"

"I was in Elm street."

"Do you visit anybody in Elm street?"

"No, sir."

"Then, pray, for what purpose were you there?"

I had taken off my bonnet and laid it on the piano; unpinned my light mantilla and pushed it back from my shoulders, to show that I understood the interview to be one of moment, and likely to last for some time. These acts helped me to gather back the self-possession I was losing, and of which I felt conscious of standing greatly in need.

"For what purpose were you there?" My father repeated his interrogatory before I could frame an answer in my mind.

"I was there to meet Mr. Holman," said I, bravely. As I thus answered, I looked at my father with a steadiness that a little disconcerted him.

"And you have the boldness to say that to my face!" he exclaimed, losing command of himself.

"I hope never to be guilty of an act that I would conceal from my father when questioned by him," was my answer. "I am not conscious of having done anything wrong."

He was too much confounded by what I had said to know how to meet the case promptly; and while he hesitated, I went on.

"Mr. Holman has communicated to me the result of his interview. While I had not ventured to hope for your approval and consent, I was scarcely prepared for the cruel manner of your denial. I did not believe that my father would wound and insult a young man who came to him respectfully and honorably, to solicit the hand of his daughter."

"Peace!" exclaimed my father, losing command of himself.

I remained silent.

"This matter must stop where it is!" He spoke resolutely.

"I am a woman, remember!" And I gave to the words all the meaning it was possible to convey in the tone of my voice. He was driving me into resolute antagonism, and I had a will equal to the emergency.

"You must give up this fellow's company!" My father spoke with just a little less of assumed authority.

Fellow! How the word quickened my heart with indignant pulses! Fellow! And applied to Edgar! This was too much. Looking steadily at my father, I replied:

"The heart does not love by square and rule,

nor ask of authority how it shall beat. It is supreme in its own world."

"Have done, will you!" He spoke very impatiently.

"You have summoned me to answer," I said, in a voice the calmness of which surprised myself. "If you do not wish to hear me, well, I can be silent."

"Self-willed, wrong-headed girl! You shall bitterly repent all this!" replied my father.

"There will come pain and sorrow, I doubt not; but never repentance." Then, after a little period of silence, I said, taking on a firm bearing, "Opposition will be of no avail, sir; the question is settled. I am betrothed to Edgar Holman; and I will keep my pledges until death. If you will not permit him to visit me here, I must submit to the humiliating necessity you impose, and meet him elsewhere—in the street, if need be."

He grew very pale instantly.

"You have driven us to precipitate avowals, and a life-compact that seems hurriedly made," I continued, "but now that we have cast the die, let me pray you to be our father, and not our antagonist; our best friend, and not our enemy. You have permitted an unjust prejudice against Edgar to come into your mind. He is worthy of your child—in all things worthy, dear father! Oh, receive him; receive him for the sake of the daughter you have loved!"

I leaned towards him and spoke in pleading tones. But he answered hoarsely, and in bitter rejection of my appeal.

"Never! The mean, sneaking wretch shall never have countenance of me!"

"He is not a mean, sneaking wretch," I replied, "but high-minded and honorable. Your daughter's choice, which will never pass to another."

"Beware, mad girl!" There was menace in my father's eyes. "I will not see myself defied and insulted by a beggarly upstart. It shall not be as you fondly imagine."

"You cannot alter what God has ordained," said I, firmly. "A woman's heart does not love by prescription. Did my mother's?" I looked with steady eyes into my father's face.

But he was blind in his disappointment. He had looked to the attainment of a desired thing in my marriage, and it maddened him to be thwarted. He had made money and position the great good; and I was affianced to a poor clerk! It was more than he could bear.

"Go your ways! Go your ways, rash girl!" he said, at length, rising and moving towards the door. "Life has always its reckoning days, and yours will come!"

I sat in tears for some time after he left the room. Then putting on my bonnet again, I went from the house, and met Edgar according to appointment.

The troubled life which I passed during the weeks and months that followed I will not describe. My father's opposition to Edgar did not in the least abate, and I had to meet him at the houses of friends or in the street—to me, often, a bitter humiliation. He would have visited me at my own home, in spite of my father's opposition, but I would not have one so dear subjected to insult; I could not bear it. My relation to Edgar did not cause me to withdraw from society, but led me, rather, to mingle in it more freely, for the reason that I often met him when abroad, but never at home.

It had become very soon apparent that Mr. Congreve knew of my relation to Edgar. He was annoyed and disappointed, and for a time kept himself at a distance, greatly to my relief. But after a while, as we met frequently in company, he gradually drew nearer again, and never seemed better pleased than when by my side. I saw this change with regret. If he had been over-intrusive, I would have firmly repelled him. But he was not. There was a certain subdued reserve about him, altogether different from the confident way in which he had sought to impress me in the beginning of our acquaintance; in fact, what I plainly felt to be an acknowledgment of my affianced position. This being so, I could do no less than treat him with that courtesy which right feeling 'dictated. He appeared satisfied with this—too well satisfied to please me. I noticed that he was on excellent terms with my father; that when they met it was with a cordiality which, to my keenly observant eyes, intimated something more than common social amenity. I did not like its aspect.

No change showing itself in my father's treatment of·our case, we fixed the time of marriage, which was about a year from the period of our engagement:

Edgar was receiving a good salary, and I was willing to try the world with him, in what some might think a humble way. The announcement was made to my father, but he deigned no response. I did not, however, fail to see that he was in a more abstracted state afterwards. We had ceased to have any controversy on the subject of my attachment to Edgar. It was useless, both saw, and therefore abandoned. No concealment of our engagement was made by either Edgar or myself, and so it became known in all the circles where I visited. No particular change showed itself in the deportment of Mr. Congreve. He was as polite, attentive, and deferential as before, but I thought a little less familiar. This seemed natural, and made me feel his presence as less repulsive. I did not like, however, his treatment of Edgar, nor his way of looking at him when they happened to meet in my presence. I had so formally introduced them, that Mr. Congreve could not help a recognition. Had he failed in respectful deportment I would have resented it, as he must have felt assured. Their conversation was always limited to cold common-places. Usually, if Edgar was present in any company, Mr. Congreve did not intrude himself upon me, except in a brief, casual way. But I now and then detected his gaze fixed upon Edgar, with an expression that sometimes made my flesh creep—it was so strange and sinister; and I felt at such times that he would do him evil if in his power.

Time passed on, with little to break the regular progression of our lives, until we came to within a month of the day fixed for the marriage ceremonial. Through Aunt Mary I learned that my father would hear no reference to the subject whatever; and refused to supply me, at her solicitation, with the money required for a bridal outfit. From her own slender means I received what was needed, and so made all preparation for the event.

About this time I yielded to a gradually approaching depression of spirits. I had felt, for some time the intrusion of a shadow upon my mind, as if an evil thing were drawing, invisibly, near. At first, this was very indistinctly perceived, but it grew more and more palpable as our appointed marriage-day came nearer. Frightful dreams haunted me in the night, so that I often came from my room in the morning pale and unrefreshed.

One evening I had met Edgar at the house of a friend, and was returning home with him. I was more depressed in mind than usual. There was on my spirit a weight as of some impending calamity. I started and trembled nervously if any one came suddenly by, or walked closely behind us. Edgar talked to me in tender assurance, and pointed my thought to the sweet, coming future. But I remained sad and troubled, even to tears.

"The blessing is too great for me," I said, as we stood, in the sad moonlight, at the gate leading into my home. "The cup too full of precious wine for mortal lips. Oh, Edgar! if it should fall, and be broken at our feet!"

"It will not, dear Edith!" he replied, with confidence. "An evil spirit, envious of such joy, is trying to make you wretched by doubts. We have Heaven on our side."

"I trust so," was my answer; yet no assurance came with his words.

"To-morrow evening I will see you at Mrs.

Darling's," he said, as he held my hands. There was a hard substance in his palm, as it pressed against mine, about the size of a silver dollar.

"I will be there, of course," was my reply. There was to be company at Mrs. Darling's, and we were invited. Then followed a kiss, and a pressure of the hand. I had scarcely any other consciousness, until I was in my room, and the token he had left with me held close to the light. My lips touched it almost as quickly as my eyes. It was a miniature of himself, in a gold medallion, wonderfully life-like. I slept with it against my heart, and dreamed for that night, sweet, tranquil dreams.

But the old pressure on my feelings came back with the morning, and I brought down a pale face to the breakfast table. The meal passed, as had become usual, in silence. At dinner-time, I noticed something unusual in my father's treatment of me. His manner was kinder, and his voice gentler. If my quick ear did not deceive me, there was a shade of compassion in his tones. I could not understand the way in which he looked at me sometimes. It excited and troubled me.

"Where are you going?" he asked, on seeing me dressed to go out, at tea-time. He seemed surprised.

"To Mrs. Darling's," I answered.

"I wouldn't go, Edith." He spoke quickly, and

with a gravity of manner that concealed, evidently, a reason which he considered conclusive.

"I have promised to be there." Very earnestly and inquiringly I looked at my father on giving this reply.

"I think you had better not go. Take my advice, for once, and remain at home." He spoke very seriously, but with unusual kindness of manner. My eyes were fixed upon him, but he did not look at me in a direct way.

"If you know of any reason why I should not go," said I, conscious, from a sense of faintness, that a death-like pallor was coming into my face, "don't conceal it from me. It would be cruel. I have promised to be there, and must keep my word, unless a barrier lies in the way that prudence warns me not to pass."

"There is such a barrier." My father looked even more serious than in the beginning.

"Then in Heaven's name, what is it?" I started to my feet, no longer able to keep my place at the table, and bent my white face, beseechingly, towards him. My father's silence, and perplexed manner, only made suspense more feeble.

"Has anything happened to Edgar?" I now demanded.

"Yes." He said it in a low voice, as if fearful of the effect.

"What of him? Speak!" I felt as if I were

suffocating. I reached out my hands, and grappled my father's garments. "Speak!" I repeated. "Speak, or I shall die!"

"Be calm, my daughter," he said. "There may be no truth in the charge."

"In what charge?" Oh, sir, if there is any pity in your heart, speak out plainly, and let me know all at once! What charge?"

I looked at Aunt Mary, but saw, from her pale face, that she was ignorant like myself.

My father now arose, and taking my hand, led me from our breakfast-room into the parlor, across the hall, Aunt Mary following. I moved like one in a dream.

"Sit down, my child. There!" and he placed me on a sofa, Aunt Mary sitting down beside me and encircling me with her arm.

"What charge, father?" I had grown calm from partial stupor of mind.

"Edgar was arrested to-day, on a charge of forgery!" The words burned like a quick fire through my brain.

"The charge is false!" I remember uttering that denial in a kind of wild phrenzy; but can recollect nothing of what immediately followed.

CHAPTER XVII.

MY mind lay for a long time bewildered in the maze of events that succeeded. I was hurt, badly, by the shock which fell upon me while in a state of highly-wrought excitement. My father knew of Edgar's arrest at dinner-time, and if he had informed Aunt Mary then, and left it to her to break the cruel intelligence in the way her woman's heart would have suggested, the effect might not have been so disastrous. As it was, I went down prostrate with the blow.

I have a dim remembrance of weeks in which I seemed like one in a nightmare, from which there was a vain effort to awaken—weeks of undefined suffering, that ached on at the heart in never-ceasing anguish.

Very clearly do I recollect the day—it was several weeks, as I learned, after my father's dreadful communication—when I found myself clothed, as it were, and in my right mind. I was reclining on a sofa, in my own chamber, dressed in a morning wrapper. I remembered getting up, and putting on the wrapper, with Aunt Mary's assistance —but as if in a dream. But now I was wide awake. Aunt Mary sat near me, with some needle-work in her hands. I looked into her face for a little while before speaking. It was greatly changed, being pale and care-worn; and there was about her sweet mouth a new expression of sadness.

"Aunt Mary!" I spoke, in a half-eager way, that I could not repress.

She dropped her work instantly, and came and bent over me, looking down into my face with a tender, yearning, pitying love, that made the tears spring into my eyes.

"Will you have anything, dear?" she asked.

"How long have I been sick, Aunt Mary?" I inquired.

"Not a very great while," she answered. "But you are better."

I did not clearly understand the meaning of her face. Putting my hand to my forehead, I tried to recall the past. It began to break upon me—dimly, at first; then distinct and startling: The anxious troubled way in which Aunt Mary looked at, and hung about me, helped to quicken my memory of the dreadful incident I have related.

"How long is it since—since?"—I could not put my thought in words; it was too shocking. But Aunt Mary understood what I meant, and replied:

"Nearly six weeks."

"O no, aunt! Not so long as that." It seemed to me, then, in my own consciousness, as if my father had spoken that blasting sentence scarcely an hour before.

"You have been sick, dear, for a long time, and are still very weak," said my aunt, in great apparent anxiety. "Don't let your mind become excited, or you will lose yourself again."

Lose yourself again! What a strange, low shudder crept along my nerves. Then I had lost myself! How many, many times since have I wished that I had never been found again.

"What about Edgar, Aunt Mary?" I spoke with a sudden flush of eagerness.

"You are too weak to talk about him now," she replied. "Wait until you grow stronger."

Wait! Tell the traveller, dying of thirst, to wait, with the cooling draught at his lips!

"I must hear now, aunt," said I. "I am stronger to hear than to wait. Edgar was charged with forgery. I remember that."

Aunt Mary's eyes were brimming with tears;

8*

and her face so sad that the very sight of it made hope expire in my heart. Still I must know the truth if I died in hearing it.

"Speak, Aunt Mary. I must know all. Don't conceal anything."

My strange calmness made her think me stronger to bear than I really was.

"Yes," she answered, "he was charged with forgery."

"But, it has not been proved against him?" I spoke in a quick, breathless manner.

"The trial will take place next month," she replied.

"Where is he now?"

Aunt Mary did not reply.

"Not in prison?"

"Yes."

It seemed as if a sword had gone through my heart, so quick and piercing was the pain.

"Mr. Congreve offered to go bail for him, but he refused to accept the favor," said Aunt Mary. "It was a kind act in him. They say that he was much affected by the unhappy event. Indeed, everybody was shocked, surprised, and grieved."

"But his innocence will appear on the trial!" I spoke in an assured manner.

"I trust that it may be so; but——" Aunt Mary hesitated.

"But what?" I asked.

"The evidence is strong against him—too strong, I fear, for any reasonable ground of hope."

I thought this sentence would kill me. I felt a dizziness of brain, and appeared to be in sudden darkness. I did not, however, lose myself.

"What do you think, Aunt Mary?" I put the question, faintly.

"You are not strong enough to talk about this now," she answered. "Don't, let me beg of you, pursue it any further."

"But, I want to know what you think." I persisted in my interrogation.

"I don't know what to think," she replied, in a reluctant and distressed way. "But you will be stronger after a while, Edith, and then we can talk more on this subject. Enough has been said now."

She was sitting near the end of the sofa on which I reclined, and her hand was resting on my forehead. Its weight seemed to oppress me, and once or twice I made a movement to push it aside, as too heavy for endurance; but the strength or will to do so was lacking, and I remained passive. I seemed to be lapsing away into unconsciousness. And it was really so, for I had not the strength of mind or body sufficient to bear the news about Edgar which I had extorted from Aunt Mary.

Again I lay in that oppressive nightmare which had been broken for a little while, and did not come back to real life until after the trial was over. Then I came back only in part; for while I understood the facts which had transpired, the knowledge thereof did not reach, with acuteness, the region of pain. My mind was dull. Its sensitiveness had departed. I did not, as at my first awaking, urge my questions upon Aunt Mary in regard to the fate of Edgar. From her manner I inferred the worst, and my inference was correct. I felt that I should know all soon enough; that the whole truth, when it came, would lie upon my heart as a burden never to be thrown aside.

This was the fact I learned :—On the trial, evidence of such an overwhelming character was produced, that no question of his guilt was left in my mind. The jury, with scarcely a pretence of consultation, rendered a verdict of guilty, and the Court considered the charge as so fully made out against him, that they awarded the heavy penalty of seven years in the State prison! Aunt Mary had given up the case entirely. All the evidence adduced she had examined with the most scrupulous care, and she was able to reach no conclusion but the worst.

I could not think of him, however, as a man who had stained his soul with an evil deed. Singular as it may appear, he was always in my imagination as innocent as when I placed my hand in his, and gave him the love of a heart that knew no guile. There lay between us, I felt, an ever-impassable gulf. He was to me as one dead. Yet I thought of him with a sad tenderness, and wept for him weak, vain tears. His miniature was still in my possession. I knew that it was something upon which no eye but mine could look without scorn; and so I kept it to gaze upon in secret. The pure, sweet, true eyes, that turned so lovingly to my face—they kept away all idea of crime. He was lost to me, I felt, yet in my heart there was no veil upon his image. I knew him and thought of him only as he had been to me in the past.

Months followed each other in a weary monotonous way. I found no interest in anything. Idly and listlessly the days passed. I would see no company, and resisted all attempts to get me out of the house for even a ride. So my life moved on for nearly a year. How patient, how wise in her adaptations to my state, how loving, was dear Aunt Mary during all this time. My father often lost patience with me, and put on a harsh exterior in his efforts to break the spell that surrounded me; but she was never changing in her love, never weary with her unhappy and often capricious charge. What she seemed most to desire, was to get me interested in doing something. Occasionally she would ask me to perform for her some little service of needlework, which I did with a ready acquiescence that I saw gratified her. The pleasure which I felt in pleasing Aunt Mary was the first available power that she gained over me. She did not use it in a way to weaken, but to strengthen it. A new request for service did not follow immediately a service performed, lest I should grow weary. And so she led me on, until I found occupation so much of a relief from dull, dreamy idleness, that my hands became busy all the day.

The first time I went out was on a mission of charity to a poor sick woman in our immediate neighborhood. Her thankful eyes were before me for many hours afterwards, and in looking at them I had my reward. I went again; and the good I was thus able to do, strengthened me for a new and better life.

I was coming home one day from a visit paid to a sick neighbor, when I met Mr. Congreve for the first time in over a year. I saw him a little way in advance of me, as I came into the square on which our house stood, and endeavored to pass without recognising him. But he stopped directly in front of me, and looking kindly into my face, said, in a tone of quiet interest, as he reached forth his hand:

"I am glad to see you out again, Miss Edith."

His manner was so respectful, so kind, and so

unobtrusive, that I could do no less than thank him for the interest he expressed, and permit him to take my hand.

" Your health is better, I hope ? " he remarked, as he still held my hand.

I said yes, only. My feeling towards him was one of entire indifference, when we first met. Not a pulse beat quicker at the sight of him. But, while he yet held my hand, and looked at me, I remembered that he had offered to go bail for Edgar Holman, and a throb of grateful emotion sent a conscious glow to my face. He could not have failed to notice the change. I now made a motion to pass on, and he bowed, respectfully, without any attempt to detain me.

As my health had begun to fail under such a long confinement to the house, and depression of spirits, my father was urgent that I should ride out with him, and get the benefit of fresh air, exercise, and change of scene. The thought of going beyond the little circle that now included my range of charities in the immediate neighborhood, was painfully repugnant; but I yielded at last to my father's continued importunity. He drove me into the country, and amid scenery that stirred many old memories—softening me more than once to tears. He tried to get me into conversation; but I had no heart to talk, and remained silent for most of the drive.

I was better for this break in the dull monotony of my existence. Again I was driven out, and it did me good. From this time, I was gradually brought into social life. I tried to resist the pressure that was on me, but was not strong enough. A few old friends came closer around me, and then drew me back to themselves. But I was not the woman of a year ago. Of that, I was deeply conscious. Life had nothing to attract me. I saw no dear hope lying even dimly visible in the far-away future. Of Edgar, I tried to think as little as possible. He was lost. That impression was one of the most distinct that remained with me. He had passed beyond my sight and reach, in an all-involving disaster, and could never be restored again. I did not, as I have before said, think of his guilt as the separating gulf that lay between us. It was simply impossible for me to believe him capable of crime. But I had no power to reason on the subject. I was bewildered whenever it came into my mind.

In going back into society again, I met Mr. Congreve now and then. He was very kind, but did not annoy me with attentions. I saw that he was not so cheerful in look or manner as he had been a year before. Often I noticed a shade of abstraction on his face which was almost painful. There was, evidently, something not pleasant to contemplate brooding in his thought.

Gradually, and by approaches so imperceptible that I did not notice them, he drew nearer to me. We met oftener than before. It happened, strangely I sometimes thought, that he would drop in where I would be spending an evening. Always at these times, he would express a little surprise at seeing me, as if he had not expected to find me there. I had reason, afterwards, to believe, that he was kept informed of these visits by my father, who, now and then, found himself unable to call for me, when Mr. Congreve became my escort home.

So the time moved on, and by steady advances Mr. Congreve continued to draw nearer and nearer. My heart was in too palsied a condition to take the alarm. I felt something of the old repulsion; but not as strong as before. In fact, I was indifferent. I cannot better express my state of mind than by these words.

Next came visits. These were at first made under pretence of seeing my father. They appeared to have some business together. Mr. Congreve was largely engaged in land speculations, and he had initiated my father into the same business, though in a smaller way. Now and then he came when my father was out, and it happening on several of these occasions that I was in the parlor, our meeting was natural.

Thus were we continually being thrown together, Mr. Congreve always showing a delicacy of feeling that made his company more agreeable than offensive.

At last I clearly understood him. What I had dimly seen from the beginning, became palpable. He came so much nearer, that mistake was impossible. Then my sluggish soul quickened into life, and I made a violent effort to disentangle myself from the gossamer threads he had been weaving around me so long, that they had become turned into strong cords. But I was feeble—feeble! Alas, for the blindness that left me to be snared by the fowler, and for the weakness of will that left me in the net!

Aunt Mary, to whom I went as my best and truest friend, counselled me right. Ah, why did I not heed her counsel? But my father was on the other side, and I yielded.

"You have no heart to give away in marriage to this man." So Aunt Mary spoke. "If you go to him, you will deceive him, and burden yourself with duties which you cannot perform. Remain as you are, my dear child. It were better, a thousand times."

But I felt that I was as nothing. That life had no blessing for me, and that it could not have, possibly, any bitterer cup than I had already drained to the dregs. If my father had so set his heart on the thing, if Mr. Congreve were so bent on gaining me for his wife, why should I disappoint them? I even argued with myself that self sacrifice in the case would be a virtue.

In my blindness and weakness I yielded. My father was very happy when consent was given; but Aunt Mary looked so sad that I pitied her.

"You take it too much to heart," I said to her. "Remember, that I am nothing in the case. It cannot make me happier or more miserable. If they desire it, why should I say no?"

"It is something to you, Edith," she replied. "Everything to you! I would rather see you die than become his wife. You cannot make him happy. It is impossible."

"It is too late now, Aunt Mary." I simply answered. And I felt then the beginning of a repugnance and antagonism which have steadily increased, until they are of maddening intensity.

Up to the last, Aunt Mary opposed my marriage with Mr. Congreve; but I had not strength sufficient to brave my father, and so went to the altar as a helpless lamb to be sacrificed.

About the time of my engagement to Mr. Congreve, I met a young man who had been a clerk in the store of Fairfield & Co. His name was Clyde. He seemed disposed to make himself familiar. I did not like him. There was a look in his eyes that always made me feel uncomfortable. Mr. Congreve knew him, I observed; but not, I inferred, as an agreeable acquaintance. Clyde often intruded upon him, I thought, judging from the expression of Mr. Congreve's face, when the young man engaged him in conversation.

The thought of Mr. Clyde came to me very frequently. Why, I could not imagine. Perhaps it was because he seemed to make himself disagreeably familiar with Mr. Congreve. I asked him once about the young man, but he seemed annoyed at the reference, and I did not intrude his name again.

Two years had passed since the separation of Edgar Holman from society, as a criminal, and I was within a week of my marriage-day. I had been spending the afternoon with a friend, and was returning home a little after sundown, when I heard the steps of a man approaching a little behind me. I was about turning to see who it was, when I heard my name pronounced.

"Mr. Clyde!" I ejaculated, with a start, as I looked back.

"Excuse me," he said, in a hesitating, embarrassed way. "But I wish to say a word to you alone, and have intruded for the purpose."

"If you can call at my father's, we can be alone," I answered, as a vague fear crept into my heart.

"I must not be seen there," was his mysterious reply. "No, I will say it here, and it is this—

don't marry Mr. Congreve. Remember, I have warned you!"

And he left me standing in such amazement, that I did not stir for some moments. This warning, given in a tone of deep solemnity, went shudderingly through every nerve. Why did I not heed it?

The incident disturbed me deeply. But I did not mention it to Aunt Mary. It would only give a new argument in her opposition to the approaching marriage, and I wished to be let alone.

"Remember, I have warned you!" I heard the injunction sounding in my ears for hours after its utterance, and with increasing, rather than diminishing, emphasis and solemnity.

I imagined, at my next meeting with Mr. Congreve, that he looked at me a little strangely and doubtfully at first. But the impression passed quickly away.

The time came down to within three days of the marriage. I was in the street, when a man passed quickly, flinging into my startled ears as he did so the words—

"Remember, I have warned you."

I knew the voice too well. It seemed as if I would fall in the sudden withdrawal of strength. But, I managed to get home, and into my room, where I lay for an hour as weak as a little child.

CHAPTER XVIII.

OST unwisely, I did not heed that warning. It was sufficient to make any woman pause and start back from a giddy height such as that upon which I was standing. Again it came to me, solemn and emphatic as at first. Only a single day intervened. The young friend who was to be my bridesmaid, had been with me all day, and left, about nightfall, to go home. I went to the garden gate with her, and stood talking there. After she left, I remained at the gate for a little while, but turned to go in as I saw a man approaching along the pavement. I was half way to the house, when the words—

"Remember, I have warned you!" were flung after me, in a deep undertone that chilled me like an Arctic atmosphere.

"What's the matter, dear?" asked Aunt Mary,

with a look of alarm, as I came into the house.
She happened to be standing in the hall.

Why did I not tell her the truth? Why did I
keep from her intelligence of that strange, repeated
warning?

I answered in some evasive way, and got up to
my room as quickly as possible. When the tea-
bell rang, I was lying on the bed in only a half-
conscious state. With an effort I aroused myself,
but felt, as I attempted to control my state of
mind, that it was too disturbed for any outward
appearance of calmness. I could not meet my
father and Aunt Mary without drawing upon me
a scrutiny that I wished to avoid, and so did not
go down at the ringing of the bell. As I expected, a servant came after a while to summon
me, but I sent word that I had a headache, and
didn't wish to eat anything.

Aunt Mary came up immediately after supper,
bringing me a cup of tea. My hand trembled as
I raised it to my lips, in spite of a strong effort to
hide the continued nervous disturbance from which
I was suffering. Very little had been said on either
side, when there was a tap at the door. A servant
had come to say that Mr. Congreve was down stairs.

"I can't see him to-night, Aunt Mary," I said.
"It is impossible! My head is aching wildly, and
you see that I am all in a tremor. I don't know
what has come over me!"

"You are not fit to meet any one, and I will see Mr. Congreve and excuse you," she replied, leaving the room and going down stairs. She came back in a little while and said that Mr. Congreve asked, as a particular favor, that I would see him, if it was only for a minute. I could not refuse what seemed so small a request, and so, making a new effort to subdue the nervous excitement from which I was suffering, I left my room and descended to the parlor.

I did not understand the quick glance that rested upon me as I came into the room. Connecting it with Mr. Clyde's warning, the sound of which had not yet died in my ears, I felt it as something strange.

"I am grieved to hear that you are indisposed." His voice was not quite clear and confident as he said this, taking my hand and drawing me across the room to a sofa which stood furthest away from the light. "Forgive me," he added, "for not taking your excuse, but I felt that I could not go away without seeing you for just a moment."

I did not say anything in reply. He looked troubled, I thought, or more like one in a state of perplexed uncertainty.

"Your hand trembles, Edith, and you are paler than usual." His manner changed to one of more anxiety.

"I do not feel at all well this evening," I made out to reply, but in a voice that no power I then possessed could steady.

"Something has happened to disturb you, I'm afraid." His look of troubled perplexity returned.

I felt impelled to speak to him about Mr. Clyde, and the words were on my lips, when some thought or impression checked the forming utterance, and I kept silence. He saw that I was about speaking, and waited for a time. Then expectancy died on his face. Our intercourse, during the short time we were together on that evening, was constrained, even to embarrassment. In all Mr. Congreve said, it seemed to me that he was feeling into my thoughts to find if something were not there which he dreaded to discover; and I, from a kind of fatal perverseness, hid what was there completely from his sight.

Mr. Congreve stayed for half an hour, and then left me. His visit tended in no way to lessen the interior disturbance from which I was suffering. Mr. Clyde's last warning had completely unnerved me. Was it any wonder? Aunt Mary was satisfied that something more than bodily indisposition ailed me, and tried in many ways to reach the true cause. But with a persistent reserve that now seems unaccountable, I kept the secret fast locked in my own mind.

My recollection of the next day—that on which

I made lip-promises to which my heart was false
—is very indistinct; more like a dream than anything else.   I have many times since tried to make
myself believe that I was neither morally nor re-
ligiously bound by the acts of that time.   They
were not done with a clear reason and free will.
I was impelled by a force too strong for any resistance that lay in me.

A marriage with Mr. Congreve did not lessen
the repulsion I had always felt towards him; and
it was not long before I let the veil drop by which
I had endeavored to hide my real state of mind.
He was kind, tender, and considerate in the begin-
ing of our inharmonious union; but my perverseness, antagonism, capriciousness, and coldness, at
last provoked him to opposition.   The prize he
had sought so eagerly as a golden one, proved of
little value in possession.   He had taken me as a
blessing, and I was already proving a curse.

My husband's large wealth enabled him to sur-
round me with every luxury.   We had, about a
mile from the city, one of the most elegant resi-
dences in the neighborhood.   I saw a great deal
of fashionable company at first; but the circle
gradually lessened, as my state of mind, from its
morbid condition, repelled instead of attracting;
and, in less than a year after our marriage, the
festive gaiety that for a time went laughing
through our house, was a thing of the past.   Mr.

Congreve was sadly disappointed. I saw this; but it in no way changed my deportment towards him.

On the birth of my little Florry, a new world of impressions was opened in my mind, and with a mother's love came the mother's joy. I began from that time to feel differently towards my husband; to find repulsion diminishing. He was very fond of the babe, and thus a new bond of affection drew us nearer to each other. But for one thing, I believe this period of my life might have been negatively happy, if I may use such a forced term. Among our occasional visitors, was the Mr. Clyde, of whom I have spoken. To my husband, I could see that he was a most unwelcome visitor; and yet he was studiously attentive to him, and exceedingly guarded in the concealment of a dislike that I knew existed. What could this mean? Why had Mr. Clyde warned me, with solemn repetitions, not to consummate a marriage with Mr. Congreve? There lay in his warning, I felt sure, a reason that would have rendered our marriage impossible, had I known it. The thought troubled me more and more, the oftener it was suggested.

I did not see in any deportment of Mr. Clyde towards myself, the smallest sign of reference to the warnings he had given. He rather kept at a distance from me; but was easy and polite when we were thrown together. He did not come very often; perhaps not more frequently than once in three or four weeks; and then he always appeared to have some business with my husband, who never seemed just like himself for two or three days afterwards.

What was the secret of his power over my husband? I could not push the question from my mind. There could be no orderly point of contact between them, I felt well assured. It was something of evil, not good, that held them in social contact. My thought brooded on the subject, and my peace was disturbed thereby.

One day Mr. Congreve was reading to me, as I sat with my baby asleep on my lap—she was nearly a year old—when our waiter came to the door, and said:

"A gentleman wishes to see you, sir."

"Who is it?" asked Mr. Congreve.

"Mr. Clyde, sir," answered the waiter.

I saw his countenance change instantly.

"Very well," he said, in a voice so different from that in which he had been reading, that it sounded almost strange.

"I wish the man were in hell!" he exclaimed, as the servant withdrew, showing a degree of passion that I had never before witnessed in him. His face had grown suddenly dark, and I felt, from its expression, that he hated this man in his very heart. The look made me shudder. There was murder in it.

In half an hour, Mr. Congreve returned to the room where he had left me. I saw a great change in him.

"I am going to the city, Edith," he said, abruptly.

"Not with Mr. Clyde?" There was so much of surprise in my voice that he seemed struck by it, and said, in a quick, sharp way—

"Why not with him?" His eyes were on my face reading it closely. There was suspicion in them.

"You don't like him," I answered.

"For all that I am going with him. He has come the bearer of unpleasant intelligence—in a business way—and I must go to the city immediately."

The tone in which he interpolated the words, "in a business way," caused me to doubt the reason they were meant to give. He did not linger in my presence, but went to his room and made a hurried toilet. Without seeing me again, he left the house and drove away with Mr. Clyde.

I puzzled myself in conjecture as to the real cause of Mr. Congreve's visit to the city, but puzzled, of course, in vain. He had given me no leading intimations, and I was, in the nature of things, all in the dark.

CHAPTER XIX.

M R. CONGREVE had been gone, maybe an hour, when I saw my father's carriage enter the grounds, and drive up the smoothly-beaten road. As it drew near, I noticed that it contained no one but his office-boy. He brought me a hastily written note from Aunt Mary, saying that my father had been taken ill, and she wished me to come without delay. Edward, the boy, could give no satisfactory answers to my questions. My father had been sick since yesterday and was worse to-day. He did not know, however, the cause or nature of his sickness, and seemed to me singularly in the dark. I was ready to accompany him in ten minutes after his arrival. My baby and nurse went with me.

I found my father in a raging fever, and delirious. From Aunt Mary's account he had been as well as usual on the morning of the previous day,

and she saw no change in him at dinner-time. In
the evening he returned later than usual, but instead of going into the office, went to his room.
He did not come down when the tea-bell rang, and
as it was an unusual circumstance, Aunt Mary
went up stairs and knocked at his door. He did
not answer at first, but on her knocking a second
time, he said that he didn't feel very well, and
would not be down to tea. She felt a little uneasy, and as he did not make his appearance after
the lapse of nearly an hour, went again to his
room and spoke to him. He replied as before,
that he was not very well. His voice did not
sound right to her ears. She asked if he would
have anything, but he said no. He remained in
his room all the evening, declining to see several
office patients who called for medicines or consultation. At ten o'clock Aunt Mary visited him
again. He had gone to bed, and replied to her
questions as to how he felt, that he had some headache, but would be well after a night's sleep.

In the morning he had not made his appearance
at breakfast-time, and on going to his room, Aunt
Mary found him in considerable fever, and unable
to rise. His mind seemed to be in a dull, confused state, as if there were pressure on the brain.
A physician was called in, who bled him immediately, and with some apparent relief. But the
fever had continued to increase, until it was vio-

lent as when I saw him. He knew me on enter
ing his room and coming to the bedside, but my
presence gave him evident pain, and excited him
in a way that had in it, to me, something fearful.
He put up his hands instantly, as if to push me
away, then covered his face and groaned like one
in anguish of soul. I laid my hand on his forehead and kissed him. But at the touch of my lips
he shuddered, and said strange words, the meaning of which I could not understand. As my
presence continued to disturb him, I went from
the room at Aunt Mary's whispered suggestion.
The sound of the closing door caused him to uncover his face, and he looked all around the apartment, as if to satisfy himself that I had withdrawn.

"Has she gone?" he asked in a whisper.

Aunt Mary said "Yes."

"Don't let her come in here again, will you?"
he said. "I can't look at her. Poor child! poor
child! it will kill her!"

"What will kill her?" inquired Aunt Mary;
alarmed by this strange language.

"Don't you know?" He looked half-wonder-
ingly at her.

She shook her head.

"Oh! I thought everybody knew it. It's town
talk by this time."

"Knew what, Doctor?"

"Is he dead yet?" My father spoke in a whis-per.

"Who?"

"Mr. Carson. Have you heard?"

But Aunt Mary knew no one by that name. He looked at her in a strange, mournful way, then shut his eyes, and lay quietly for a long time. When I again ventured into the room, and he be-came aware of my presence, he grew excited as before, and resolutely hid his face from me. All this was dreadful! What could it mean?

"Won't you take her away?" I heard him whisper to Aunt Mary, who led me from the room again. When I ventured in once more, after half an hour had gone by, I found him in a heavy stupor, with his face so dark that it was almost purple. His appearance alarmed me greatly. The physician in attendance called again at this time. I saw by his countenance, the moment his eyes rested on my father, that his symptoms had changed for the worse. He said something in a low tone to Aunt Mary, who went from the room and called Edward. In a few moments I heard the boy's rapid feet going down the path to the garden gate. He had gone for a consulting physi-cian. But it was too late. When he arrived, my father's condition was hopeless. He died that night; the physicians said from apoplexy.

I had left word for Mr. Congreve to come for

me, on his arrival at home, and I was surprised, and a little troubled, that he did not make his appearance during the evening. In the morning, I looked for him early, but he did not arrive until long past noon. An exclamation of surprise fell from my lips on seeing him, he was so changed.

"Are you sick?" I asked.

He said "Yes," in a strange, evasive way, his eyes glancing past mine, instead of into them.

"This is very dreadful, Edith," he added, before I could make inquiry as to what ailed him.

"Why did you not come last night?" I inquired. "I looked for you every moment."

He answered that it was after dark when he got home, and he felt too unwell to ride back to the city. I was not satisfied at his late appearance that day. He had been too sick, he said, to leave home earlier. But I afterwards learned, incidentally, from a servant, that he had not been home all night, nor until past meridian of the day succeeding that on which my father died.

I was a great deal shattered by this sudden death of my father, around which, to me, there dwelt a dark mystery. There was, I felt, something more than apoplexy, as a simple disease, involved. Antecedent to the physical disease was some fearfully exciting mental cause. What was it? How was it connected with me? Over these questions, in the darkness that followed, I brooded like some night-bird.

After my father's death, Aunt Mary came to live with me. Mr. Congreve was a different man from what he had been. In all my strange moods and capriciousness, he had, for the most part, treated me with a kindness that ever sought to win the love he must have been too conscious of not possessing. But now, I saw indifference and coldness creeping over him, yet without concern. I had never loved him. Not once, from our marriage-day till now, had my heart beat a single true throb for him; and I felt that estrangement on his part would be sweeter to me than loving attentions. He had committed a great error in constraining me into a marriage that he knew was in opposition to my feelings; and the fruit of that error had been bitter to his taste from the beginning. It was yet to become as gall and wormwood!

I saw nothing more of Mr. Clyde. If he still continued to annoy Mr. Congreve—and it was plain that he had active sources of annoyance—he did so by letter, or personally in the city, whither Mr. Congreve went every day.

"I'm afraid," said Aunt Mary, about this time, "that things are getting wrong with Mr. Congreve. Has he said anything to you about removing from here?"

I replied that he had not.

"He more than hinted as much to me, yesterday," continued Aunt Mary.

I was in no way disturbed by the suggestion. In fact, I had grown weary of the life I was leading, and felt a restless desire for change. I had, long ago, ceased to find any pleasure in the external of things around me; and in new conditions, no matter what, there was a suggestion of relief from a dull monotony that was eating into my very soul, and destroying the little vitality that remained. I was not, therefore, in the least disturbed, when Mr. Congreve said to me a few days afterwards:

"Edith, circumstances have occurred that will make it necessary for us to remove from here. I am sorry to have you disturbed in your pleasant home; but necessity knows no law."

I saw that he was surprised, as well as greatly relieved, that I made no objection.

"Do we go to the city?" I asked.

"No," he replied.

"Where?" I queried.

"East, probably."

This surprised me.

"To the East!" I said. "Why to the East?"

"Business will require me to go there."

"Soon?"

"Immediately." His manner was disturbed,

and he did not, while talking with me, look, ex
cept for a moment at a time, steadily into my
face.

"Where do you think of going?" I asked.

"To New York, in all probability; but I cannot as yet determine. I have found a gentleman
who would like to purchase this property. He
will take everything—furniture and all, as it
stands; and that will save us the unpleasant notoriety of a sale and break-up. We can pass
away as quietly as though going upon a summer
tour. You will like that best, I know."

No arrangement could have been more agreeable. On the next day, Mr. Congreve brought out
a man who looked through the house and over the
grounds. I was informed, after he went away,
that he had agreed to purchase.

"How soon can you get ready to start for the
East?" was Mr. Congreve's inquiry, on the evening of that very day.

I said in a month; Aunt Mary mentioned two
or three weeks; but Mr. Congreve said—

"You must be ready to start in a week from
to-day."

"That is simply impossible," I replied.

"What is to hinder?" he asked, showing considerable impatience.

"I have no travelling dresses," was my answer.

"Buy them to-morrow, and have them made up. A week is long enough to get an outfit for travelling the world over."

I objected, but Aunt Mary came in, as usual when a difference occurred, and told Mr. Congreve that if it was of importance to get away at the time stated, she would undertake to have everything ready.

"It is of the first importance," he replied.

The week that followed I passed in a whirl of busy preparation for our hurried flight. I often questioned with myself as to its meaning. It was plain enough, from Mr. Congreve's manner, that something of a serious nature had occurred. He was never still, it seemed, for a moment, when at home, but went restlessly about the house, or over the grounds, often in an absent way, that showed a mind in troubled abstraction. He slept but little through the night, frequently leaving his bed and walking the floor. Every day he went to the city, from which he rarely returned until late in the afternoon.

The morning of the day fixed for our departure had come. Trunks were packed, and nearly everything in the way of preparation completed. The house was to be left in the care of servants, who, on our retiring, became, according to arrangement, responsible to the family by which we were to be succeeded.

We had left the breakfast-table—Mr. Congreve, Aunt Mary, and I—and were sitting in one of the smaller parlors that looked out upon a lawn and garden, talking over some last matters, when a man stood suddenly at one of the French windows, and pushing it open, stepped into the room.

I gave a short, low cry, as I recognised Edgar Holman; changed, oh, how sadly changed! but with a face as familiar as though I had looked upon it only a day gone by. He came a few. paces into the room and then stood still. His air was that of a man trembling in some eager impulse, yet irresolute as to action. Mr. Congreve was sitting in a position that enabled me to see his face, when he saw and recognised Edgar. He grew deathly pale, but did not stir. His lips fell apart, and his eyes stood out like one transfixed in sudden terror. I could neither move nor speak.

The first moments of surprise over, Mr. Congreve started up and exclaimed:

"How dare you come here, sir?" His face was still white. I saw him thrust his hand into his bosom as if searching for a weapon; but happily none was there.

"I can dare anything for justice and retribution!" he was answered, and in a voice so calm and stern, that it seemed to push Mr. Congreve from his feet, for he sat down again in a weak, nerveless kind of way.

"And that time has now come," added Mr. Holman, as he took a chair, in a deliberate way, that stood right in front of us.

"I am at liberty again, you see, Mr. Congréve," he went on; "and not only at liberty, but with all the proofs in hand to establish my innocence and your guilt. Did it never occur to you, sir, that there was a God in heaven? I fear not, or .you would have hesitated."

Mr. Congreve was on his feet once more. But Mr. Holman fixed his eyes on him, and held him as still by his gaze, as an animal is sometimes held.

"Sit down again, sir." The tones in which this was said were scarcely above a whisper, but they were like the pressure of a giant's hand on Mr. Congreve.

"You wrought hard to prevent my pardon by the Governor, and I do not wonder. But the proofs of innocence were too strong, and here I am! Why, it is not needful I should say. You know full well. Frederick Carson did not die without making a sign, for all your efforts to the contrary. He could not venture into the next world with the guilt of perjury, unconfessed, upon his soul, though you would have sent him, without a throb of pity, to eternal ruin, in order that your work might be covered from human sight. But that was not to be! He died—and his testimony remains. John Clyde—Yes, sir, you may well start at the name! Accomplices in crime are rarely disinterested parties. You should have remembered that evil tools are sharp, and may cut both ways. John Clyde is revengeful as well as venal. He had you completely in his power, and the temptation to exercise that power on one whom he had reason to hate, was too strong to be resisted. They say that revenge is sweet to the wicked, and he is tasting this wild honey.

"But I must be explicit, for I speak to other ears. There was a maiden's heart all my own— pure, true, and sweet as spring's first blossoms. You could not rob me of the heart: it turned from you with instinctive loathing, as an angel turns from a demon. And so you plotted to destroy me. A corrupt young man, a fellow-clerk of mine, was bought with your money—I use plain speech—and induced to personate me in a forgery. John Clyde accomplished his work most skilfully, and then perjured himself to make my ruin complete. Poor Carson, more weak than wicked, was bribed heavily to swear that I bought a watch at a store where he was salesman; and he even produced similar bank bills to those paid by the teller on the forged check, and afterwards found on my person, in evidence of my guilt

The web of circumstances woven by you and Clyde so skilfully, it was not in my power to unravel. But I never wholly despaired. I did not lose all faith in God and justice, dark as was the night in which I had to sit down, and long as it continued before there came even a dim precursor of morning.

"It has broken at last. But what wrecks do I see as tokens of the storm raised by your infernal incantations! Poor, miserable Carson, repentant but cowardly, gave out just enough of the truth to make an application to the Governor for a pardon successful. You discovered what was in progress, and tried hard to obstruct a movement that was setting in the right direction—but tried in vain. The terrors of fast-coming death were more potent than any influence you possessed—I am well posted, you see, sir—and the dying man made a full confession. How fatal did it prove to one, at least! He made it to Dr. ———, and the horror of mind occasioned thereby, led to brain fever, apoplexy, and death. I don't wonder at your quivering nerves and ghastly paleness. Your enemy has found you out, and he will not spare."

I don't know how it was that I was able to sit calmly and hear all this. But while my ears drank in every word and believed it, my heart kept its even beat. He went on.

" I am here now to claim her who should have been my lawful wife. To take her from the prison of your arms. To bear her away from one who has cursed her life. Edith ! "

He uttered my name in a kind of suppressed cry, rising and holding out his arms. I did not think, nor pause, but sprang into them, and felt myself clutched to his breast !

CHAPTER XX.

KNEW nothing of what immediately followed. When thought took up the thread of consciousness again, I was in a strange room, lying upon a bed. I believed myself alone, at first, but in the dim light of the chamber, soon saw Aunt Mary sitting by a table engaged in writing. I observed her for some minutes in silence, and then made a slight noise to attract attention. She left the table at once and came to the bedside.

"Can I get anything for you?" she asked. I did not observe any surprise in her manner at seeing me awake. The impression on my mind was that of a person just aroused from sleep.

"Nothing," I answered. I now saw that she began to look at me a little more curiously.

Again I surveyed the room, trying to make out some familiar article, but was unsuccessful.

"Where am I, Aunt Mary?" I arose and leaned on my arm.

She put her hand on me quickly, and showed some excitement of manner.

"Lie down, dear. You have been ill, and are very weak."

It needed not her words to signify that I was but a child in strength, for the slight effort of rising up caused a faintness to come over me and I sank back on the pillow. After lying, with closed eyes, for a few moments, still retaining clear consciousness, I repeated my question :

"Where am I, Aunt Mary?"

"You must not press that question now, dear. When you are stronger, I will answer."

I was not, of course, satisfied with this reply. But I felt too weak to press the matter; and closing my eyes again, tried to think back to the last incidents that were impressed on my memory. It was not long before that never-to-be-forgotten appearance of Edgar Holman was recalled in all its startling particulars. His arraignment of my husband, and distinct recitation of circumstances by which his own innocence was attested, and the guilty complicity of my husband affirmed, were all before me. I remembered every emphatic word, and the effect also. In my mind Edgar stood fully justified; and in these first minutes of returning consciousness, I lifted my heart and thanked God that it was so.

"We are not in M———? " said I.

My voice was calmer than my feelings.

"No, dear; but you must not talk now." Aunt Mary laid her fingers on my lips; but I pressed them gently aside, and put the question:

"Where is Mr. Congreve?"

"Here," was answered.

"And Edgar?"

"I do not know, Edith." Her countenance began to grow anxious and troubled.

"What happened, Aunt Mary, after—after—?" I could not say what was in my thoughts, but she understood me.

"You must wait until another time—until you are stronger, Edith."

I still questioned, but she would not answer explicitly. While we yet talked, the door opened, and Mr. Congreve came in. I gave a short cry of repulsion, and covered my face with the bed-clothes. The very sight of him filled me with fear and hatred. He came to the bedside, and after saying a few words that I did not hear to Aunt Mary, went out.

" Has he gone?" I asked, uncovering my face.

"Yes," she replied.

"Don't let him come in here again, I can't bear it." My manner was disturbed.

Aunt Mary only sighed. I continued:

"Tell him, will you, that I hate him."

She laid her fingers over my mouth, but I pushed them off. I was growing more and more excited every instant.

"I hate and loathe him!" I flung out the words with all the emphasis my weak state permitted. "He is not my husband; but a fiend who thrust himself in between me and the man to whom my heart was, is, and will be for ever married."

I had risen up, in the wild passion of the moment; but the strong fire burnt itself out quickly, like flame in a gauzy scarf, and I fell back again into unconsciousness.

I did not ask, when thought and feeling returned, how long I had remained in happy oblivion. I was in the same apartment, with Aunt Mary. Florry sat on the floor, playing with some toys, and singing to herself in a sweet, low voice, that came pleasantly to my ears. She looked strangely matured; and I could hardly credit my eyes, when she got up from the floor, and walking firmly across the room to Aunt Mary, asked her a question in a voice that articulated each word distinctly. At this moment, the door was quietly opened, and before I saw who had come in, Florry clapped her little hands and uttered the word "Papa!" Mr. Congreve then stepped into full view. It seemed as if a horrid demon had come into my presence; and as he reached out his hand to take my child I gave a shriek of involuntary terror. Mr. Congreve started, and putting Florry down hastily, came towards the bed; but I lifted my hands and cried out—"Keep off? Don't touch me!" in such a mad way, that he stopped at some paces distant, turned about, and left the room.

I was trembling all over when Aunt Mary reached me. She drew her arm around my neck, and bent over me with a hand on my cheek, which she moved in the caressing way that a grieving child is sometimes quieted. Florry, who had been frightened by my sudden scream, now came clambering on to the bed, and nestling close against me. How her little hands, as they touched my neck and bosom, sent electric thrills to my heart!

"Is this Florry?" I said, as her lips came sealing themselves upon mine, and her golden curls covered my face.

"Yes, ma'am, I'm your Florry!"

What did all this mean? I thought, for I had never heard that voice, in clearly spoken words, before; I could not make it out.

Exhausted by the wild passion into which I had been thrown, I found myself so weak that I could only lie still, with shut eyes, and think feebly. Florry's head was close beside mine on the same pillow, and her hands in my bosom. Aunt Mary tried to remove her, but I drew my arm and held her to her place.

As I lay there, all the desolate heart-aching past came out of the darkness, and spread itself before me, even to that maddening revelation which fell from the lips of Edgar Holman. From that period, though many months had passed, all was a blank.

I did not, then, say anything to Aunt Mary, though a few questions were revolving in my thoughts and restless for solution. I resolved to wait for a little while—to try and be calm, until more strength was received. I kept this resolution for an hour, perhaps, when I could no longer repress a single query.

"You must give me a direct answer to one question," I said.

"What is it?" Aunt Mary raised a finger to her lips as she spoke.

"Has any harm come to Edgar?"

The answer was unequivocal—"No."

That was a great relief. I closed my eyes and lay for some minutes.

"Where is he?" was my next inquiry.

"I do not know."

"Have you seen him since that day?"

"No."

"Nor heard of him?"

She put her finger on my lips and said:

"You asked for one direct answer, and I have given you three. I must keep you to your own stipulation; or rather, from exceeding it any further."

I shut my eyes again with a sense of relief. No harm had come to Edgar. "Thank God!" I said in my heart, fervently. There was hope in the world yet; I would live for him.

" Aunt Mary, one thing more."

She shook her head.

" If you desire for me life and reason keep that man away from my presence. The sight of him fills me with anguish and hatred. If I had the strength I would flee from him to the uttermost parts of the earth."

Aunt 'Mary regarded me with a sad countenance, but made no reply. She left me alone with Florry, a little while afterwards, and remained away from the room for nearly a quarter of an hour. I heard, now and then, the murmur of voices in a distant room, and guessed that Aunt Mary was using her influence with Mr. Congreve to keep him, at least for a time, away from my presence. She was successful. I did not see him again while I remained in that room.

Gradually, strength began to return. In a week, I was able to sit up in a chair for half an hour at a time, once or twice during the day.

Then I was able to get to the window and look out—a thing I had greatly desired. Aunt Mary had informed me that we were in Pittsburgh, whither we had come on our way eastward. I had no recollection of the journey.

In three or four weeks I was strong enough to ride out. I felt desirous to recover my strength, and willingly accepted the means that were offered. There was a new and precious hope in my heart—it is there still, an undying thing—the hope of meeting Edgar; of meeting him and being united. For this, I consented to live. Without it, I would have died long ago.

"I think," said Aunt Mary one day, "that you are now well enough to resume the journey your illness required me to suspend."

I made no objection. The only concern I had was the fear of meeting Mr. Congreve during the journey, or on its termination. That he was not far distant I had many evidences. I did not see him, however, during the long ride to this city. The house at the corner, to which we were brought, had been furnished, and there were servants ready to receive us. It was, I understood, to be our future home. A day or two passed without the appearance of Mr. Congreve, when, as I stood at the windows, looking into the street, I saw a carriage stop at the door. He had arrived! I ran up stairs to my room, and locked myself in, all trembling with excitement. After a while, Aunt Mary came and asked to be admitted. She brought a message from Mr. Congreve, who desired to see me; but I refused him in the most positive manner.

"Remember," she said, in her remonstrance, "that this is your husband's house."

"He is not my husband!" I cried back, half madly. "I reject the relation! That marriage was a fraud!"

"Don't speak in this way, my child," replied Aunt Mary. "It is sinful."

"The sin rests with him, not me," I answered, resolutely.

"You must see him, Edith. He is in earnest, and will take no denial."

"I will *not* see him!" My heart was growing strong within me. "Tell him that I hate him; and that if he approach me, I will flee from him as from my worst enemy."

Aunt Mary might as well have talked to the wind as to me.

All day I remained in my room alone with Florry. She asked, many times, that I would let her go and see her papa. But I would not consent. Twice, during the afternoon, he came to the door, and demanded that I should open it. But only the room's dead silence echoed his demands. I did not let even a whisper escape my lips; while, with a raised finger and look of authority, I kept my child voiceless, though tears ran over her scared face.

At last, he made an attempt to force the door, and succeeded. But as he entered, I, losing all thought but that of escaping his detested presence, caught Florry in my arms, and made for the open window. He seized my garments in time to prevent me from throwing myself and child headlong to the pavement. You saw my little one in convulsions that evening, and now know the cause!

Since that time Mr. Congreve has steadily persisted in attempts to bend me to his will; but he might as well attempt to bend an iron girder. He has cursed my life, and that of one who is dearer to me than life. Have I not reason to loathe him, and to hate him? I have; and I do so loathe and hate him, that his presence either suffocates or maddens me.

He is hiding himself here at the East from the sure retribution that is on his track. The plea of business is only a subterfuge. Edgar, if living, will never give up the pursuit. How long his coming is delayed! The wonder to me is that Mr. Congreve has not already been arrested for the crime that blackens his soul. I fear that he has compassed, in some way, the death of Edgar Holman. Sometimes this idea gets possession of me so strongly that I lose myself. I could not live, if I were certain that he were dead. If I knew where he was, I would go to him. I have said so to Aunt Mary over and over again, and I will keep my word if ever that knowledge comes.

Mr. Congreve came back yesterday, after a longer absence than usual. I had begun to hope that he would never return. When he came under the roof that covered me, I passed from beneath its shelter, and I will not go under it again while he is there. Do not fear, my kind friend, that I mean long to trespass on you. This I have no right to do. But let me hide myself here for a little while. If he stays long, I will find another place of refuge from his presence.

And so you have my wretched story; and I know from your face that it has given you, as I said it would, the heartache.

CHAPTER XXI.

SO much of the mystery was explained; but it brought us, as it were, into the very heart of an unfinished drama, or tragedy it might prove, with the action still in progress. And it was impossible to hold the position of mere spectators—to sit quietly in the boxes and look on. We must take our places on the stage and become actors in at least some of the scenes that were to follow.

"What are we to do in this matter?" My wife put the question with a sober face. Mrs. Congreve had positively refused to return home while her husband was there.

"I think," was my answer, "that our duty is a plain one. Mrs. Congreve's story has given us facts that alter our relation entirely. On Edgar's account we have a personal interest in her, and for his sake, as well as for humanity's sake, we must do all in our power to save her from the mental ruin towards which she is now tending. We must let her stay here as long as she will, and make her feel that she is fully welcome."

"If she knew our personal interest in Edgar," said my wife, "it would give us more influence with her."

"For the present," I replied, "we must keep our knowledge of him a secret. She is the wedded wife of Mr. Congreve, and, as such, cannot, innocently—cannot, I mean, if in a sane mind—entertain the feelings and purposes which she avows in connexion with Edgar. The shock she has received, and the extraordinary trials which she has endured, have weakened her mind. Feeling has been intensified, while reason and judgment have been enfeebled. She must be guarded and guided in the perilous way her wavering steps are treading, and to you and me, providentially, has been assigned the duty of helping her to walk in safety along the Valley and the Shadow of Death through which her soul is passing."

"Poor Edgar! I cannot think of him and the past five or six years of his life without shuddering. I wonder where he can be, and why he has not written to us?"

"One thought, probably, absorbs him," I answered; "the thought of retribution. He is, I do not question, in the pursuit of this man, who has managed so far to elude him."

"But this cannot long continue. He must find him out."

"Yes, and speedily. If alive, he may appear on the stage at any moment. Wo may look for him daily."

"He may not be living," said my wife. "Do you think a man like Mr. Congreve would stop at murder when so much was involved?"

"In murder all is jeopardized. It is a fearful stake, and the worst and most daring may well hesitate before casting it down. I hardly think that extremity has been reached in this case."

"Then it is strange that Edgar has been so long in discovering their residence here. They could not have left their home in the West so secretly that no one knew of their departure or the direction. It would seem to be an easy thing to trace them as far as Pittsburgh, and thence to this city."

"It is probable," said I, "that Pittsburgh was reached by a very indirect way. Mr. Congreve may have taken at first, a different direction, and Edgar may now be hundreds or thousands of miles distant, in a vain pursuit. But no matter what the cause of his absence, Mr. Congreve cannot escape him in the end. This great sin will not go unpunished. I feel sure of that."

"What if Mr. Congreve should come here and demand his wife?"

"I should still leave her free to go or stay," was my answer. "So long as she desires an asylum here, she can have it."

"Can he not remove her by force?"

"No. She is as free, personally, in the eye of the law, as he is."

"I mean," said my wife, "on the allegation of insanity."

"He will scarcely take that step," was my answer.

I was mistaken here. I was informed that a gentleman had called to see me. No name was given; but on going down into the parlor, I recognised Mr. Congreve. He mentioned his name, and said:

"I am your neighbor at the corner."

I bowed, and requested him to resume the seat from which he had risen on my entrance. He looked very serious, and his manner was that of a man laboring under considerable mental excitement.

"My wife is here." He spoke abruptly, and with a resoluteness of manner that I saw was meant to impress me with the idea that he was a man not to be trifled with—at least not in the present case.

"She is." I tried to speak in a voice that would show firmness, but not indicate antagonism.

"Will you say to her that I wish to see her?"

Now this was bringing on the issue at once. I knew that she would not see him, and I knew, still further, that to take this message would be to excite her mind in a way dangerous to its rational balance. I could have gone from the room under pretence of carrying his request to Mrs. Congreve, and brought back to him words that she had spoken in the most emphatic way to my wife, but this involved subterfuge, and I would not consent to that.

"I think," said I, "that you had better not disturb her this evening."

"And why not, pray?" He was very imperative.

"Perhaps," said I, assuming a rather more decided manner, "your own thoughts will suggest a reason."

His brows drew down suddenly, and his eyes gave a quick flash, as he returned:

"You speak in a riddle, sir."

"No," I answered calmly, "not in a riddle; but if obscurely to your thought, I can be more explicit. I hardly think it required, however."

I fixed my eyes so steadily upon his face, that his half-insolent gaze was turned aside.

"This is very extraordinary!" he said. "I can't understand it."

I made no response to these ejaculations.

"Then you will not even say to my wife that I wish to see her?"

"I only suggested that it were better not to disturb her," said I. "If you insist on having your desire communicated, I cannot, of course, refuse."

"Then I do insist upon it."

I left the room and saw my wife. After a hurried consultation, she went to Mrs. Congreve, who, on learning that her husband had called and wished to see her, became very much excited, refusing, of course, to meet him.

"Tell him," was her reply, "that, if I can prevent it, he shall never look into my face again."

I did not change, in a syllable, this message.

"It is well," he said, showing less disturbance than I had expected.

He then added:

"Of course you have not failed to see that her reason is disturbed?"

I assented, unwittingly.

"In other words, and speaking in direct language; she is an insane woman. I had faith, if I could have gained an interview, in my ability to persuade her to return home. Failing in this, I must place her under constraint. It is the last resort; and I would delay it still longer, if possible. But this step, and *your evident concurrence therein*"—he put an emphasis on the last words—"make my duty clear. If she will not remain under her husband's protection, she must be cared for in another way. An insane woman cannot be permitted to go at large."

He arose, and stood, for a few moments, with something irresolute in his manner.

"I must caution you," he said, "against putting too implicit faith in any statements she may, in her confusion of thought, be led to make. She has taken up some extraordinary hallucinations."

"I can and will make all allowance for the unhappy state of mind from which she is suffering," I replied.

He stood silent again for some moments, and then said:

"I cannot help expressing surprise, sir, that you, as an entire stranger to me and my family, should be so ready to take the responsibility of interference in a matter about which you are wholly ignorant. I am not used to having my path crossed in this way; and do not find it in the least agreeable."

"There has been no interference on my part, sir," I answered. "Your wife came here in a most unhappy state of mind; and we have done all in our power to calm her excitement, and restore the mental equipoise that has been sadly disturbed. We gave her quiet and seclusion. No neighbor, that we are aware of, knows of her presence in our family. If she had been our own sister, we could not have treated her more kindly, or with greater consideration. Have you, then, a right to complain of us? I think not, sir! Passion and force are not the means of restoration in a case like this. There must be a course of wise conciliation. And you must pardon me for saying that if I am to judge from your temper to-night, you have not always pursued this course towards the woman who has fled from under your roof. I speak plainly, sir, for I think it best in the outset that we should understand each other."

"In the outset of what?" demanded my visitor.

"Of an intercourse which does not promise to begin and end to-night," I replied.

He looked at me sharply.

"You are a bold man!" he said.

"I am a resolute man," was my simple answer.

"I am puzzled to know what interest you can possibly have in this affair," he remarked after a while.

"I have an interest in it, notwithstanding," I replied.

"You! What interest, pray?" His manner was a little startled.

"Enough to make me oppose any attempt to remove Mrs. Congreve, against her will, from under my roof. And I suggest, now, that you give up at once all thought of placing her in an asylum, as I infer you have intended doing."

He grew pale at this remark.

"So long as she is content to remain here you had better permit her to remain," I added.

"Most extraordinary!" exclaimed Mr. Congreve, in a perplexed, half angry voice. "I can hardly believe my own ears. It seems that you, an entire stranger, have constituted yourself an umpire in my affairs, and now stand ready to enforce your decisions. I cannot accept your interference, sir, and I will not."

"You state the case too strongly, Mr. Congreve," said I. "This thing has been thrust upon me. Providentially I have been drawn into a relation with your wife which makes a certain care for her a common duty. And when I see a duty clearly, I am in the habit of compelling myself to go forward in its performance, in the face of all consequences. And I wish you to understand that there will be no holding back in the present case. My advice to you is, to treat me as a friend, and not as an enemy. You will accomplish far more by acting in concert than in opposition. Consider my house an asylum, if you will, and your wife in durance here. I will hold myself accountable to the last particular for her safety."

Mr. Congreve turned from me abruptly, and

walked the full length of the parlor two or three times.

"More extraordinary still!" he ejaculated, stopping before me at last. "I cannot make it out. What possible interest can you or yours have in Mrs. Congreve?"

"There is the interest of common humanity," I replied.

"I don't believe in it! Wouldn't give that for common humanity!" and he snapped his finger and thumb contemptuously. "All talk. There is more beyond."

He threw the short sentences out impulsively.

"Perhaps there is," said I, thinking it well to warn him.

He started a little, and again I saw a paler hue on his face.

"I see," he said, "that nothing is to be accomplished to-night," and he made a movement to retire. "You have assumed a serious responsibility, sir; and one that may bring you into trouble. I am not a man used to having my path crossed; nor one apt to forgive. If I am not always a warm friend, I pride myself on being a bitter enemy. You have put yourself in antagonism with the wrong man, and I warn you to re-adjust your position, and that right speedily!"

He stood regarding me for a few moments with a malignant gleam in his dark, evil eyes, and then went out hastily. I do not think he saw any sign of fear or wavering in my face.

CHAPTER XXII.

DID not think it well to alarm my wife by repeating all the threatening intimations of Mr. Congreve. It would only create uneasiness of mind, without doing any good.

Mrs. Congreve did not show any strong interest in the fact of her husband's visit. He was so hateful to her, that she did not care to speak of him.

"You needn't tell me," she said, "if he comes again. I wish to be as one dead to him. I am only sorry that he has annoyed you, that his breath has polluted the air of your home; but I will not trouble you long."

In the morning Aunt Mary came in with little Florry. She mentioned that Mr. Congreve had gone away soon after breakfast, saying that he would not return for a week. This information caused Mrs. Congreve to go back to her own house.

When I learned this fact I was relieved in

mind. I took it as an indication that Mr. Congreve had been influenced by my resolute manner, and would, for the present at least, refrain from all compulsory measures in regard to his wife. During the short period that she was with us, she remained in a tolerably tranquil state. My wife, even in this time, found her heart going out towards her with an unusual tenderness; and Mrs. Congreve was already leaning upon her and confiding in her with something of filial confidence.

"It is very clear," said my wife, "that for some good end we have been brought into this close and confidential relation to Mrs. Congreve. I feel it more and more sensibly every day. She needs a friendly interest such as we have begun to feel; and counsellors such as I trust God will give us the wisdom to be."

"Great prudence must be exercised on our part. Edgar will find her out, and then ——"

"What then?" asked my wife.

"Ah, that is the difficult question. If he is of the same purpose now as when he gained that first interview with Mrs. Congreve, there will be a state of things hard to keep in a right moral adjustment. But the way, I trust, will be made plain for all of us."

"When a wrong path is entered," said my wife, "what human foresight is able to reach the possi ble termination?   Such paths never lead to happiness."

"Never," I replied; "and yet the world takes them with a blind folly that is inconceivable. The father of Mrs. Congreve was, we may suppose, a man of ordinary intelligence in the common affairs of life—had, in most things, a discriminating mind; yet what fool could have acted with a madder insanity!   Did he love himself or his child most?   Ah, it was his self-love that blinded him to her good; that made him fill the cup of her life with gall.   He knew from reason, observation, and written life-histories, that the most wretched of all women are those unhappily married; and yet he literally forced his child into marriage with a man who was, as he had every reason to believe, loathed in her heart.   Could such seed produce anything but a harvest of misery?   And was there any guarantee that himself would not be one of the reapers?   The misery came too surely; and he had to gather his garners full.

"And Mr. Congreve.   How the law of cause and result, with the quality of the cause active in the result, has been proved in his case.   He sowed the wind, and verily is he reaping the whirlwind!   To gain, by unfair means, or through wicked devices, is not really to possess.   What looked like gold in the distance, turns, in all such cases, to some worthless substance in the hand, that wounds and poisons it, mayhap. Mr. Congreve has fully illustrated that old fable of the physician king. Tantalus-like, he is athirst, with cool water below and around him; an-hungered, with fair fruit bending in luscious sweetness from full boughs overhead; yet, when he stoops to drink, the waters recede from his lips—when he stretches forth his hands, the full laden branches lift themselves beyond his grasp."

"If in his folly and wickedness, he had cursed no heart but his own," said my wife in some bitterness of spirit, "we might think of his suffering without regret. We might even feel glad in his pain."

"No," I remarked, "not glad, but sorrowful. Pain of any kind, bodily or mental, is a thing to excite our pity, not our joy."

"I spoke from indignation, and that is oftener cruel than merciful," was answered. "But we are only human, and the heart will rebel."

"Think and feel as we may," I said, "pity those who suffer the consequences of their evil ways, or rejoice in the sure retribution that has found them, the law that makes pain the certain accompaniment of wrong done from a bad end, will ever act with unerring certainty. The bad man's enemy, pain, will surely find him out."

"And the good man's friend, delight, find him out also."

" Just as surely," I replied.   " The law works in either case without variableness or shadow of turning."

" Do you think," said my wife, " that Mr. Congreve will make any serious attempt to get his wife into an asylum? The thought every now and then flits through my mind and troubles me. He has reason enough for wishing to remove her from all intercourse with persons in the neighborhood."

" There is no way that he can do this that I can imagine. If she were in the habit of riding out with him, or with any friend in his confidence and willing to act with him, it might be an easy thing to drive her to an asylum and leave her there. But as she never goes out riding with any one, the difficulties in the way are almost insurmountable."

My wife's mind seemed rather more at ease on this subject after we had talked it over, and looked at it from all points of view.

One evening—it was the third or fourth from that on which I had received a visit from Mr. Congreve—Aunt Mary came in. It was between nine and ten o'clock. She had evidently, from the expression of her face, a purpose beyond a mere call; and both myself and wife waited in expectation of some request, or communication of interest. Nearly five minutes passed in ordinary conversation when Aunt Mary said:

" You wished to see me ? "

" No, no."   Aunt Mary's countenance changed, and she spoke quickly:

" You sent word for me to call in."

" Who by ? "

" I don't know. Somebody came to our door and said that you wished to see me."

" I sent no such word," replied my wife.

" It's strange."   Aunt Mary had risen, and her face was looking slightly alarmed.   " You are certain you did not send for me? "

" Positive."

" I can't understand it. What can it mean?" Our visitor stood with a perplexed manner for a little while, and then added: "I must run home again. Edith was asleep on the sofa when I left."

I took up my hat to accompany her home. She objected, saying that it was only a step, and she would not trouble me. But I felt a vague suspicion that something was wrong, and I went with her.

" What does that mean !" she exclaimed, as we reached the pavement.

I turned my eyes towards the corner. There was a carriage at the door, and I saw, indistinctly, a man enter it. Then the carriage started, the horses moving with a sudden spring, and whirling away, passed out of sight in the darkness before we reached the spot on which it had been

standing. The door of the house stood wide open.
As we entered, I detected the smell of ether.
Aunt Mary ran up-stairs swiftly, and I heard her,
a moment afterwards, calling in an alarmed voice
for the servant. The girl answered from one of the
rooms in the third story.

" Where is Mrs. Congreve?" asked Aunt Mary,
as the servant came down stairs.

" She's lying on the sofa," replied the girl.

" No, she's not in the room where I left her."

" Maybe she's gone to bed," said the girl.

" No, she's not in her chamber. Who came in
that carriage?"

I had gone up-stairs, and now stood in the passage on the second floor. The servant looked bewildered at these questions, and in a hurried,
alarmed voice, said:

" I didn't see any carriage, ma'am," she replied.
" Nobody's been here."

" Somebody has been here! I saw a carriage
drive away, and found the front door open.
Edith!" Aunt Mary called the name in a quick,
eager manner. But there came no reply.

" What strange odor is that?" she turned her
ashen face upon me.

I did not reply that it was ether. She was
alarmed enough already.

" When did you go up-stairs?" Aunt Mary
spoke to the servant.

"Just after you went out," she replied.

" Was Mrs. Congreve asleep on the sofa, then ? "

" Yes, ma'am."

" Who told you that I had been sent for ? "

" A girl came to the door, ma'am, and said you were wanted in there for a little while."

I looked narrowly at the servant as she answered these questions. Something in her manner did not satisfy me.

" You heard a carriage drive away just now ? " said I.

" I heard a carriage," she replied, " but didn't know it was from our house." Her eyes were not lifted from the floor as she answered me.

We now went to the sitting-room. As I entered, I noticed that the smell of ether was stronger here than in the passage. There was no doubt on my mind as to what it meant. The truth had flashed on me the instant I perceived the peculiar odor mentioned. Mr. Congreve, or some one employed by him, had entered the house soon after Aunt Mary left, and by means of ether produced unconsciousness in Mrs. Congreve, and then removed her, noiselessly, to the carriage! The truth, I saw, had now reached the thought of Aunt Mary ; for she sat down in a feeble way, and looked into my face despairingly.

" Do you think *he* has done this ? " she asked, in a choking voice.

"There is no doubt of it," I replied.

"For what purpose?"

I did not answer.

"Where is Florry?" Aunt Mary started up suddenly.

"She's all right, ma'am! She's in her bed," said the servant in a positive way.

"How do you know?"

"Oh, I'm sure of it, ma'am."

But no assurance, except that of her own eyes, could satisfy Aunt Mary. She ran over into the chamber where the child slept, and found her there.

I noticed this positive manner in the servant, and yet she had not been in Florry's chamber since she came down-stairs. How did she know that the child had not been taken away with the mother? I felt suspicion against her increasing in my mind.

What was to be done? Our case seemed, for that night at least, helpless and hopeless. Edith had been spirited away in the darkness, and there was no sign as to the direction which had been taken. Pursuit, for the time being, therefore, would be a vain effort, and was not attempted. In my own thought there was no question as to the agency at the work and the purpose in view. Mrs. Congreve would be removed to an insane asylum, in order to prevent communication with my family, and with any other persons to whom she might be led to speak of things that were likely to involve her husband in serious consequences. My greatest anxiety was for the effect on Mrs. Congreve, when she awakened from insensibility. I feared this shock would complete the ruin of an already disturbed intellect, which, under right influence, might have been restored to its normal condition.

Nothing could be done for that night. My wife remained with Aunt Mary, and I lay awake in perplexed thought pondering the uncertain work, and doubtful result, that were before me on the next day.

CHAPTER XXIII.

N the morning early, I took a horse and buggy, and drove to the Insane Asylum, located about two miles from the city. I did not know the Superintendent personally; but his reputation as a wise, humane, and honorable man, precluded all question as to his right conduct in the case of Mrs. Congreve, should she have been placed in his care. He was above the suspicion of being accessory to any scheme of iniquitous incarceration. If I found her there, I did not doubt of my ability to secure her almost immediate dismissal. But on gaining an interview with the Superintendent, I was satisfied that Mrs. Congreve was not there. I explained to him the way in which she had been removed, and described her person, so that if she were brought there during the day, he might understand the case, and treat it with the judicious care it required. He seemed indignant at the outrage which had been committed, and said, that if the object were to give to a temporary aberration of mind a permanent condition, no surer way could have been adopted.

During the day I communicated with the Chief of Police, and in the afternoon visited the asylum again. But I could learn nothing of Mr. Congreve. I now began to fear that she had been taken from the city by one of the early morning trains. The probability of this being done had been suggested to my mind on the night before, but I had reasoned against it on the ground that such an attempt would not be made, as Mrs. Congreve, on becoming sensible, would violently expose her husband. He would not hazard, I had said to myself, the doubtful experiment of conveying her from the city in a car or steamboat. Now, it occurred to me, that he might have rendered her partially stupid by drugs, and while in this condition removed her without attracting attention.

I returned from my late afternoon visit to the asylum, in a troubled and despondent state of mind. The twilight was falling as I stood at my own door. In going through the hall, I noticed, in a side glance, a man sitting in the parlor. I kept on to the end of the hall, where I removed my hat and coat.

"Who is in the parlor?" I inquired of a servant.

She replied that she didn't know. The gentleman had asked for my wife, but on learning that
she was out, had asked to see me. He had not
given his name. I learned from the servant that
my wife was still absent. So I went into the parlor to see who was there, and what the visitor
wanted.

The man arose, in the twilight of the room ex-
tending his hand, and calling me by name. I
took the offered hand, and strained my eyes in
the dusky atmosphere, but could not make out
his face.

"You don't know me, I see," he remarked.

I now detected something familiar in the voice.
My eyes were getting used to the feeble light in
the room, and I perceived his face more distinctly. I had seen the lineaments before, but where
and when I was not able to recal.

"You do not know me," he repeated, seeing
that I continued to look at him in a doubtful
way.

"My memory is certainly at fault," I answered.

"I am changed since we met last, and not much
wonder." His voice fell to a low key. "I am
Edgar Holman!"

My hand closed on his with an eager grip. Till
then, it had been lying loosely in my clasp, as
when he laid it there.

"Oh, Edgar!" I exclaimed. "It is you indeed!"

He had not, evidently, anticipated anything so cordial as this recognition, nor would he have received it but for my full assurance of his innocence, gained through the story of Mrs. Congreve.

"Yes, or at least what is left of me," he replied.

We sat down, face to face, and I looked at him attentively. The old expression and the old outline of his countenance were gone. I would scarcely have known him. He had passed through the fire, and the signs of its terrible power were visible.

"Alice is not home," he said.

"No," I replied. "She is in at one of our neighbors; but will return soon."

It then occurred to my mind, that it would be best for me to see my wife first, and take a little counsel with her in regard to Edgar, so I added:

"If you will excuse me for a moment I will go for Alice."

I found her with Aunt Mary, who was waiting in a most anxious state of mind for my arrival, hoping that some intelligence of Edith would reach her through me. But I brought her neither light nor comfort.

The few moments of hurried thought I was able

to give to the subject, led me to the conclusion
that Aunt Mary ought now to be made acquainted
with our relationship to Edgar Holman; and also
with the fact that he had arrived at this most important crisis. His aid in discovering Mrs. Congreve would be invaluable. Yet the question as
to whether he should be informed on the subject
was the one of most difficult solution. In approaching the matter with Aunt Mary, I said:

"You are aware that Mrs. Congreve related
her history to my wife?"

"Yes," she answered.

"And that we have shown a very decided interest in her?"

"Yes."

"An interest that may have occasioned you
some surprise."

"It has. We were only strangers, and in a
doubtful attitude."

"There was a reason for it," I said. "She
had a miniature clasped in her hand on the night
we found her so near to the door of death. I
saw the face, and so did my wife, on that occasion."

"It was the miniature of Edgar Holman," said
Aunt Mary.

"And Edgar Holman is my wife's cousin."

Aunt Mary laid her hand quickly across her
bosom, and looking at my wife, said—

"Can that be possible ! "

"It is even so," she replied.

"And I have one more communication to make. He is here ! "

"Edgar ? " exclaimed my wife.

"Yes, Edgar."

"Where ? "

"At our house. I found him there on my arrival at home, just now."

The new complication of affairs which this appearance of Edgar was likely to occasion, suggested itself to both Aunt Mary and my wife, and kept them silent. Their minds seemed to be in a maze of doubt.

"I mention this now," I said, "in order that we three may take counsel on the subject before my wife sees her cousin. The question is, shall he be informed of your proximity, and the existing state of things. My own mind is not clear."

"Better wait for a little while," replied Aunt Mary, without hesitation. "Listen first to what he will relate, and gain from what he says some knowledge of his state of mind. We can then more easily decide what it will be right for us to do."

I saw that this was the correct view, and at once assented.

We found Edgar in a feverish state of mind. He had arrived from the West that afternoon

11*

and was in pursuit of Mr. Congreve, having got upon his track after being for months baffled by false indications, which led him always in an opposite direction from the true one. He related the story of his love for Edith, with a tenderness of feeling that melted us to tears; of his arrest, trial, condemnation, and long imprisonment, with such vivid portraitures of his agonized mental state, that we seemed to be passing through the fiery trial ourselves; of his fierce indignation against Mr. Congreve when the full knowledge of his complicity became known to him, in such strong words, that we found ourselves carried away by his wild spirit of vengeance.

How weak I felt before this strongly agitated man, with the memory of such cruel wrongs spurring him on, single-handed to retribution; and yet my duty was to lead him to a better way than the one he was dashing forward in with headlong fury. How was this to be done? I felt so weak, that I prayed for wisdom and strength. I looked upwards, and said—"Lord teach me!"

As we sat together on the next morning, I said:

"This deep provocation, Edgar, has blinded your reason. You do not see clearly."

"I have not pretended to see for some time," he answered. "I only feel."

"We must walk by sight, if we would reach the goal of our wishes; not with shut eyes, nor in the darkness. No real good is secured, if sought in violation of human or divine laws. The wrong you have suffered, cannot be righted through another wrong."

"The wrong is too great," he answered, "for adjustment by ordinary modes of redress. Mr. Congreve has removed the question from judicial grounds, and now it is only to be settled at a higher-law tribunal."

"There are two commandments," I said, "which are included in both civil and divine codes, by which external and internal order are maintained. Now you, in the blindness of passion, deliberately propose to break one or both of these laws. There is murder in your heart, and there is, also, the firm intent to possess yourself of another man's wife. I put the issue in words without disguise."

"She is not his wife," Edgar answered indignantly. "He gained possession of her through a wicked fraud. Her heart is mine, not his."

"She gave her hand to him," I replied calmly, "of her own free will, and promised to be faithful to him before God and man. He is legally her husband, and he is also the father of her child. Here are the plain, ultimate facts, which cannot be altered. Do not, let me conjure you most

solemnly, attempt to go past them. You and
Edith have been wretched enough in the past;
do not make the future doubly wretched."

He did not answer for some time after I made
this appeal. At last he said, taking firm hold
upon my arm, and speaking in a voice from which
the late fierceness was gone—

"I have had no counsellor but my own wildly
throbbing heart, and maybe that is leading me
astray. It would be no wonder!"

"It is, Edgar—assuredly it is! Lean on me
for the present. Trust in me. Be patient and
enduring for a while longer. Day-dawn has come
after the black night season, and the morning
will break. Oh, wait for the morning—wait in
the patience of hope, that when it comes, it find
not all the ground desolate."

He seemed much softened by this appeal, and
I went on, trying to lead him into a better state,
where rational thought could have power over
him, and I was in a small degree successful.

Edgar only knew that Mr. Congreve had come
East. Beyond this, he was yet uninformed. There
did not seem to be in his mind the remotest idea
of the family's immediate proximity.

For months, since his release from prison, he
had been an excited wanderer from place to place,
his mind eager in the pursuit of one object. There
had been no rest, no opportunity for reflection,

no retreat from the outside world, into which he could retire, and find calmer influences than those by which he was surrounded. He had, in a word, no home. In supplying these, we gained just so much on the right side. ' He had turned aside from the world, and entered the sphere of home, and I could see that its power over him was felt.

The closer I observed him, and the more I thought upon the subject, the clearer it became that he must not be informed of what was then passing. A knowledge of the fact that Mr. Congreve had carried off his wife, and that she was now, in all probability, in some mad-house in the vicinity, in danger of becoming a confirmed maniac, would have set his whole being on fire. He would have become doubly desperate. And so, greatly as we needed his aid—greatly as we might have profited by his undying ardor in the case—we dared not let him into the secret.

Securing his promise to remain with us for a few days at least, and without making any attempt to prosecute his searches in our city for the present, I left Edgar with my wife, and started forth early, to obtain, if possible, some intelligence of Mrs. Congreve. As she had been taken away in a carriage, I set on foot, through aid of the police, inquiries among hackmen, with intimations of a reward; but up to the evening of the second day, no one was found who would admit having been employed on the occasion of Mrs. Congreve's forcible removal. Two other asylums were visited, but without finding the object of my search.

What was to be done? Every passing hour made the danger to Mrs. Congreve more imminent. If reason were not already permanently dethroned, the utter prostration of her mind was almost inevitable, if a much longer time elapsed before her restoration to Aunt Mary and her child. By aid of the telegraph and police, I had made inquiries in neighboring cities; but so far without any result.

"This last act on the part of Mr. Congreve," said I to Aunt Mary, as we sat in gloomy conference that night, "throws him beyond the pale of consideration. He has gone a step too far, and risked too much. We must give this matter to the public by advertisement, let the consequences be what they may."

She did not reply immediately. The suggestion was new, and she was giving it some consideration.

"What good will follow?" she asked, at length.

"It may lead to the discovery of Mrs. Congreve."

"And, at the same time, expose everything to Edgar," replied Aunt Mary. "Is there not more to be lost than gained?"

"The greatest loss is Mrs. Congreve's reason," said I.

"No." She simply uttered the word.

"What greater loss in this case?" I askod.

"Can you not see?"

I signed a negative without speaking.

"There is something of higher account than reason. A stained soul is more to be dreaded than a shattered intellect. It may be as well that Edith was removed just at this time. She is not strong enough to hold back should Edgar reach out his arms for her with the passionate appeal he once made. Attracted on one side so strongly, and repelled with equal force on the other, she would have no adequate power of resistance. Poor child! poor child! It were better, perhaps, that the worst we have feared for her should take place. I could accept that before the other and more direful consequence."

This was taking a new view of the case, and one against which I offered no argument.

"You think, then," I said, "that public notoriety should for the present be avoided?"

"Under the circumstances, I do."

"In the nature of things, Edgar cannot remain very long in his present ignorance," I suggested.

"No; but we can wait until the veil shall fall of itself, so to speak, or in better words, until Providence shall permit it to fall. That, let us believe, will be the best time. For the present, when all is dark before us, we had better keep back our rash hands."

"There is reason in what you say," I remarked. "But if inaction is to be added to suspense?"

"Let us do what we can in the way our best judgment dictates," said the even-toned woman, "and try to have patience for the result. There is a way above our ways—a Providence that works beyond men's evil deeds to the accomplishment of the highest remaining good. Our dear Edith is in the hands of One who will not depart from her, even in this hour of darkness. He will preserve in her that which is most precious and eternally enduring. I rest the matter here in unwavering confidence. I have no other hope, and cling, in my weakness and sorrow, to this."

I answered nothing. What could I say?

"In patience and hope for to-morrow," I said, as I held her hand in parting that night.

"There will be a to-morrow," she answered, yet her lips quivered, and her eyes were full of tears.

CHAPTER XXIV.

O-MORROW came, but not in sunshine. It opened on a day as dark as the previous one had been. Not a sign came to our troubled, waiting hearts. I spent the greater part of it in fruitless efforts to gain some intelligence of Mrs. Congreve.

Edgar, after his long, eager, passionate state of mind, had fallen into what seemed more like stupor than calmness. He sat brooding, rather than thinking, for hours at a time. After relating to us, in all the fervor of a life-realization, the sorrowful story of his past, he scarcely referred to it again.

On the third day, he went out for the first time. We felt anxious lest he should meet the truth we were trying to conceal from him, face to face. But we had come, to some extent, into Aunt Mary's state of mind. The power to determine results according to our own judgment was not with us; and so we tried to wait patiently, and in the belief that all things would work to the best termination under the circumstances.

"It is night—dark night," we said. "But the earth is revolving, and morning is on its way."

In the evening, as we sat talking, Edgar said abruptly:

"Who lives in the corner house?"

My heart gave a sudden throb, for I perceived in the tone of his voice, a concealed interest in the question. Now, there was more than a single corner house in our neighborhood. Where two streets cross each other, there are usually four corner houses. So I answered, while my wife's eyes rested a little anxiously on my face—

"A Mr. Wetmore," giving the name of a gentleman who lived opposite the dwelling which Mr. Congreve had taken.

"Why did you ask?" I inquired, seeing that he made no further remark. I was too desirous to know the reason why he had put the question to leave the matter in suspense. He answered, without much apparent interest in his tones:

"I thought I recognised a face at the window."

My wife and I exchanged startled glances.

"The name is Wetmore, you said?"

"Yes."

"It was the house on this side of the street and at the nearest corner," remarked Edgar. Now

Mr. Wetmore lived, as I have said, on the other side of the street. My cousin looked at me, as if for confirmation in regard to the occupancy, by Mr. Wetmore, of the particular house he had designated. I let my eyes fall away from his, and did not answer his questioning look.

"It was very much like her face," he said, after a while, speaking partly to himself.

"Like whose face?" asked my wife, who felt as I did, that something must be said, lest silence should awaken suspicion.

"Like the face of Edith's aunt. I saw it for only a moment, receding from the window, and turning from me in what I have thought a hurried way. But fancy may have deceived me; and it is not the first time." Both Alice and I looked away from Edgar. We feared that our countenances might betray us.

"There was a child at the window, also," said Edgar, " and it had a countenance like sunshine for beauty and brightness. I stopped to look at the rare, sweet face, and caught the image in my mind. I am not apt to be struck with children's faces; but this one impressed me in a peculiar way, and moved my feelings as if by a strain of old familiar music, heard after the lapse of years."

He fell away into a state of absent-mindedness, from which we did not seek to awaken him. He was about recurring to the incident again, when I turned his thought, by a question, into some other and safe direction.

On the next day, business took me into a part of the city far distant from that in which I lived. It was at the northern side, and near the suburbs. The man I wished to see lived in one of six rather ancient-looking houses, some of which had been modernized by new fronts, and other showy improvements, while three or four of them retained all the unsightly marks of time and not very careful usage. These had heavy wooden shutters to the third story, the large black iron bolt giving them a prison-like appearance. On the opposite side of the street were six more of the same style of houses, showing much the same contrast between advancement and retrogression.

After finishing my business with the person upon whom I had called, he walked to the door with me, and we stood there conversing for some minutes. As I parted from him, and walked down the marble steps that led from his door, I noticed a small slip of paper, to which a narrow piece of black ribbon, not over two inches in length, was attached, fluttering down in the air, which was a little disturbed by wind. It fell upon the pavement a little in advance of me, and I was about passing it, when an impulse of curiosity induced me to stoop and pick it up. It had evidently been torn from the fly-leaf of a book, and in a hurried manner. The edges had a fresh appearance, as if the rent had just been made. The piece of ribbon was not cut at the ends, but ragged; and the hole in the paper through which it had been passed, had plainly been made with the fingers. But there was no ink or pencil mark on the paper, nor any scratch formed into an intelligible sign. Only a few pin-holes were visible; but I could make nothing of them. It looked like a child's work done in aimless play, and I was about throwing it down as a thing of no significance, when I changed my purpose and thrust it into my pocket.

My thought went away from the little slip of paper almost as soon as it was out of sight, but returned again in a few minutes. I took it from my pocket and looked at it again. The little perforations made with a pin, or some sharp instrument, now struck me as being more numerous than at first sight. But after examining them for a few moments, I crumpled the paper in my hand, and was about casting it from me, when a different impulse led me to place it again in my pocket.

I had to walk for a distance of several blocks before reaching a street railway line. As I took my place in a car, this suggestion crossed my mind.

"That piece of paper may have been a signal from Mrs. Congreve!"

For a moment or two I dwelt upon this, and then pushed it aside as improbable. But it returned after a little while, and held, for a considerable time, possession of my mind. I had heard of such things as private asylums for the insane, or of such persons as powerful relatives might have an interest in secluding.

The thought dwelt with me so steadily that I determined to call on Aunt Mary and show her the trifle I had picked up. She looked at me expectantly as I came in, but I shook my head, and met the question she would have asked with the words:

"No news."

She sighed deeply, and in a disappointed way. I then took the bit of paper and ribbon from my pocket and handed them to her without speaking.

"What is this?" she asked.

I did not answer. She looked at them closely. In an instant I saw her face change.

"Where did you get this?" There was a low thrill of eagerness in her voice.

"I picked it up in the street."

She held it to her eyes again with a more careful scrutiny.

"Edith had on a mourning collar with a piece of ribbon in the edge just like this!"

"Are you certain?"

"Very certain."

It was difficult for either of us to repress the excitement we now felt.

"Let us examine the paper more carefully," said I. "There are pin marks all over it."

We brought it close to the light. At first we could make nothing out of these minute perforations. But we soon saw that they had a certain regularity.

"There is E, plainly enough! Can't you see it?"

Aunt Mary's eyes were quicker than mine. Yes. I saw it now. The letter E had been punctured by a pin or needle.

"And that is E! E C!"

"Edith Congreve!" The words fell from me as we looked at each other in sudden astonishment.

"You picked this up in the street?" said Aunt Mary.

"Yes. It came down to me, fluttering in the wind, and I lifted it with no thought of its true significance."

"Did you see the house from which it came?"

"No. But it was from one of twelve. I will return there immediately."

"Go—go quickly!" exclaimed Aunt Mary. "The signal may be repeated. I am sure it was from Edith. If she saw you once, she may see you again.'

Without waiting for a longer conference, I started forth, and taking a car, was soon on my way back to the neighborhood I had just left. There were in the block, as I have said, twelve houses. Originally, they had been built with heavy white shutters, from the first to the third stories. But about half of them had been altered in this particular, and the lighter Venetian gave to them a less prison-like aspect. By contrast, the others were now gloomier, and more suggestive of warehouse contents than the faces of happy wives and children. On reaching the square, which was flanked on either side by these grim-looking dwellings, I ran my eyes in a rapid way along the dingy fronts, from house to house, with a kind of vague expectation. But the house gave no sign. Not a shutter moved, not a face appeared, no hand threw me a quick signal. I walked slowly along one side of the street, affecting not to be on the lookout, but with my eyes making quick passages from window to window, running backwards and forwards, up and down, like the fingers of a skilful player on the keys of an instrument. Then I crossed over and walked in the same way on the other side of the street. But to no better purpose.

Three times was this done, the same result following. In two of the prison-like houses on one side of the street, and in one of them on the other side, the shutters of the second and third stories were just a little bowed, as the ladies call it. In the others, they were as tightly closed as if the houses were tenantless. I conjectured that in one of the houses with the bowed shutters, Mrs. Congreve was confined, and I kept upon them, for the most part, my watchful eyes. But all proved in vain. Fearful of attracting a suspicious attention, I was about leaving the neighborhood, and had turned to walk away, when on throwing back a last glance, I noticed a small bit of paper floating down upon the air. It was midway between the houses, and when I first saw it, higher than the second story windows. It fell near the centre of the street, and at some distance from where I stood. My heart beat rapidly. Here was, I doubted not, another signal from the imprisoned lady. I marked the spot where the paper fell, and then glanced from house to house to see if any one was observing me, or in a condition to observe me, should I attempt to get the little missive into my possession. No one being visible, I walked back along the pavement, until I came opposite to where the bit of paper lay, and was turning off from the pavement, when I heard a shutter pushed open just above my head. I glanced upwards, and the face of a woman looked down upon me. It was a hard, sallow, sinister face, and the eyes, as they rested for a moment on mine, had, I imagined, something evil in their look of quick inquiry.

Passing on, without securing the piece of paper, which I saw had a bit of black ribbon attached to it, I walked on as far as the corner and then crossed over, so that I could see the house opposite to which it was lying without turning purposely to do so. The shutter which had been pushed open, remained partly unclosed, and I saw the woman's head just far enough advanced to give her a good line of observation, up and down the street. Instead of returning by the other side, which would have been to draw the woman's more scrutinizing eyes upon me, and create suspicion, if there existed in her mind any ground of suspicion towards a too curious stranger, I passed the corner, along a cross street, and so out of the range of her vision.

In about ten minutes I returned by the same way. As I regained the corner, from which, at a glance, I could see the house before which the object I was so anxious to obtain lay, I saw that the shutter which had been opened so untimely, was closed. Quickly crossing to that side, and moving down to the point I wished to reach, I saw the bit of paper lying just where it had fallen. In an instant it was in my possession. I did not examine it until I was in the cars, on my way back.

It was very similar to the piece of paper which

I had picked up only a short time before, and had evidently been torn from a fly-leaf of the same book from which that had been torn. The two or three inches of black ribbon were broken off at the ends, instead of being cut, and the hole in the paper, through which it had been passed, was evidently one made with the fingers. Little perforations covered the face of this bit of paper, as they had covered the one previously obtained. But I was at fault as before; I could not make out any form of letters. For nearly the whole distance of my long ride in the cars, I endeavored to wrest from those little pin-marks the important secret they kept too well; but all to no purpose. The perforations were so few and far apart that I was unable to connect them.

Aunt Mary's eyes were soon added to mine in the scrutiny. I expected her to read the signs at once, but after puzzling over them for ten minutes, she could only make out E C, and that did not unravel half that was written, or rather punctured. The form of every letter in the alphabet was applied to the irregular series of dots, but we could make no correspondence with either. At last Aunt Mary exclaimed:

"They are not letters but figures! This one is 5."

I saw the form, as with a pencil she united the points by dark lines.

"What is the next?" I said, all in a tremor of nervous excitement.

We were at fault only for a few moments.

"It is the figure 4," said Aunt Mary; and her pencil made it clearly apparent to our eyes in a moment.

"And now for the next!" I could not repress my eagerness. Before Aunt Mary had made out the last figure I saw the outline.

"It is 2!" I exclaimed. "542! The very number of the house from which that bad face looked out upon me with such a sharp expression. I noted it down as I passed."

CHAPTER XXV.

EDITH is there!" said Aunt Mary, as we read with undoubting clearness, the initials and figures "E C, 542." In the ardor of examination she had remained singularly composed, but now she was trembling all over, and beads of sweat stood on her pale face.

"She is there, without question," said I in response. "Mr. Congreve has, in order to baffle our search, placed her in a private house."

"What will you do?" asked Aunt Mary. "How can you get her from this prison? If you fail in the first attempt she may be taken beyond our reach."

"I do not mean to fail," was my encouraging answer. "When I return to that neighborhood, it will be in the name of civil authority, and with civil power at my right hand."

"Can you secure this?" she inquired anxiously.

"Without doubt!" I spoke in the most assured manner. "The Chief of Police is interested in the case, and when he learns that Mrs. Congreve is in all probability confined in the house I will point out to him, I can answer for his prompt action. She will be restored to us, I trust, in less than an hour from this time."

"Oh, sir, do not delay a moment!" said Aunt Mary, laying her hand on my arm. "Go—go—and quickly! Even now, suspicion awake, they may be removing her."

I said what assuring words I could find, and was going down stairs, when my wife, whom I had not seen since morning, pushed open the street door, and came in quickly. She had a partly folded newspaper in her hand. On seeing me she cried out in a voice full of excitement—

"Oh, husband! Have you heard of it?"

"Heard of what, Alice?" I saw something in her face that I did not understand.

"About Mr. Congreve!"

"No; what of him?"

"What of him?" echoed the voice of Aunt Mary behind me.

"Edgar saw it in the paper a little while ago."

"Saw what, Alice?" I spoke almost impatiently.

"He is hurt badly, and the paper says cannot live! There was an accident in the cars."

"Where?"

"Near Baltimore. But here it is."

I took the newspaper from the hand of my wife and read aloud:

"Fatal Accident.—This morning, as the train from Washington was within half a mile of Elk Ridge Landing, an axle of the last car broke, and the car becoming uncoupled, was thrown from the track. One man, Mr. Dyke, of Missouri, was killed, and two others so badly injured that they cannot possibly survive. Of the wounded men, we could learn the name of only one. That was Congreve, a gentleman of wealth, formerly residing in the West. One of the passengers fully recognised him. His injuries are of an internal character, and it is said that he cannot possibly recover."

"Can it be," said I, turning to Aunt Mary, "that this is the husband of your niece?"

"Heaven knows," she answered, through blanched lips, tremulously.

"Edgar will know of a certainty," said my wife, "for he is already on his way to Baltimore; or at least on his way to the cars that will take him there to-day."

When, a little while afterwards, I parted from my wife and Aunt Mary to visit the Chief of Police, and get his efficient aid in the work of recovering Mrs. Congreve, I felt that the knotted skein of her unhappy life was about to be untangled. The concurrence of events seemed too remarkable for any other anticipation. And yet, while all lay still in darkness and uncertainty, a heavy weight rested on my feelings. It was only conjecture that Mrs. Congreve was in the house number 542. The evidence, at first sight, was conclusive; but so much was at stake, that my heart from hope went down into anxious doubt, and from doubt went up to confidence again, so alternating at every step of the way in which I was passing forward.

After I had related to the Chief of Police all that the reader knows, and showed him the bits of paper I had picked up, he called one of his deputies, and asked him who lived in the house number 542 H—— street. · The prompt answer was—

"Dr. T——."

"I thought so," replied the Chief.

"You know him, then?" I said.

"Yes; I know the man very well. He's a physician of some previous reputation, but not much in practice now; at least not in an active city practice. He receives patients into his house more frequently from a distance. They are usually treated for some form of insanity."

" Judiciously treated ? " I asked.

" I cannot say anything to the contrary," was replied. " Nothing that demanded our interference has before occurred; and now there is no evidence of bad treatment. The lady is only detained against her will."

" Against justice and humanity as well ! " I declared warmly.

The Chief only bowed.

" You say," he remarked, " that this lady's aunt, with whom she was living at the time of her forcible removal, is not only anxious for her restoration, but ready to attest the cruel wrong that the act of removal involves."

" Yes, yes," I answered.

" Then it will be well for me to see her, and best, perhaps, that she accompany us to the house."

" Shall I call a carriage ? " I asked.

The Chief assented. The deputy entered with us, and we drove to Mr. Congreve's house. There a brief interview was held with Aunt Mary, and the Chief of Police being entirely satisfied, requested her to accompany us, which she did.

Half an hour brought us to the locality before described. I suggested that we should leave the carriage, when in the neighborhood, and approach the house on foot.　But the officer understood his own business better than I did, and let the driver rattle up to the very door, which opened almost as soon as we reached the pavement—that is, three of us.　The deputy had orders to remain in the carriage.

With the air of a man on business, the officer ascended the steps, we following.

"Is Doctor T—— in?" he asked of a woman who held the door partly open, putting his hand upon it as he spoke, and pushing it back.

I heard an affirmative answer.　The officer then passed in, Aunt Mary and I close after him. The woman showed us into a parlor that was well furnished and apparently well kept.　A few choice pictures hung on the walls.

"What name?" asked the woman.

I gave my name, knowing it would be an unfamiliar one to the doctor.

We sat for three or four minutes, when a short, stout, firm-looking man entered.　His complexion was fair, and the heavy beard that covered his mouth and chin·a little mixed with grey.　His eyes were small, dark, and full of quick intelligence.　The expression of his face was pleasing rather than repulsive.　He bowed and smiled on meeting us.

"You have a lady under your care," said the officer, speaking at once, and in a quiet but self-possessed way, "that we wish to see. Her name is Mrs. Congreve."

My eyes were fixed upon the doctor's face. A kind of pleasant surprise came into it.

"Are you not mistaken?" he returned, with a smile.

I felt my heart sink heavily. We had been deceived in our conjectures! It was plain to me that Mrs. Congreve was not there.

"I believe not," replied the officer. "The lady may not be here *as* Mrs. Congreve; still the one we seek is in your house. A pale lady in black. Her aunt wishes to see her."

The smile went out of the doctor's face. I saw that and took hope again. He did not answer immediately. I waited for his words, holding my breath—so did Aunt Mary.

"You speak in a positive way, sir."

The officer bowed. His eyes were upon the Doctor, whose manner lost just a shade of self-possession. It was recovered again immediately.

"If I had a lady patient under my charge answering to your description, I should require, for her production, something more than the simple demand of a stranger."

"Of course," said the officer, quietly taking from his pocket a small gilt token of authority and attaching it to the breast of his coat.

The doctor's manner changed instantly.

"The lady was taken from her home forcibly—abducted, in other words—and you, in becoming a party to the matter, have incurred a serious responsibility."

"I had the certificate of her family physician as to the state of her mind, and the necessity for treatment," the doctor replied, thus admitting the important fact that Mrs. Congreve was in the house. He spoke in an assured way.

"Who was her physician?" I asked.

"I do not now remember the name. But the certificate is in my possession. I am particular in regard to all these matters."

"Can we see the paper?" said the police officer.

The Doctor went to a secretaire in the back parlor, and taking from a drawer a small bundle of papers, selected one and brought it forward. The officer examined it for a moment and then handed it to me. I saw that the name of Mrs. Edith Congreve was in the document. The signature, with an M.D. attached, I did not know. Silently, I passed it to Aunt Mary.

"It is a forgery," she said, promptly. "No such physician is known to us—no such physician was ever in our family."

"This has a bad aspect," said the officer, as he took the paper from Aunt Mary's hand, and reached it to the Doctor. "Such things cannot be done with impunity in this city while I stand at the head of its police. Let us see the lady at once."

He spoke tho last sentence in a tone of authority not to be misunderstood.

"Come, madam," he added, looking towards Aunt Mary, who rose to her feet instantly.

"Show us to the lady's apartment." The officer was moving towards the door. Doctor T—— made no further opposition, but led the way up stairs, we following. On reaching the third story, he called a female attendant, who sat in a small room sewing, and directed her to show Aunt Mary into the front chamber. The woman drew a bunch of keys from her pocket, and unlocked the door, opening it only part of the way. Aunt Mary passed in, while we stood waiting on the outside.

I heard a quick, glad exclamation in a well known voice. Yes, Mrs. Congreve was there. In three or four minutes the two ladies came out, both in tears and strongly agitated. I grasped the hand of Mrs. Congreve, and looked earnestly into her face. She uttered my name, adding:

"Oh, sir; I am your debtor more than tongue can tell!"

There was no wildness in her manner, nor other evidence that her reason had been seriously disturbed by the outrage she had suffered at the hands of her husband. My heart beat lighter as I saw this.

We did not linger on the way down-stairs, but passed out quickly, and in less than half an hour Mrs. Congreve was safely in her own home, nothing the worse, as far as we could see, for the excitement, fear, and painful suspense of the last few days.

CHAPTER XXVI.

HE newspapers on the next morning brought intelligence of Mr. Congreve's death. He had lived only a few hours after the accident. An undertaker went on to Baltimore, and had the body properly interred in Green Mount Cemetery.

On the third day after his hurried departure, Edgar Holman returned.

"It was mine enemy," he said, as he reached out his hand to me. "I looked into his face, and was satisfied."

"He is dead," I remarked.

"Yes; and gone to his reward. He cursed my life; but I do not think his was any happier in consequence, or will be through the interminable ages. Let him pass now. He is out of my way, and I would that the memory of him might depart from me for ever. But where is Edith? I could learn nothing of her or Aunt Mary. They

were not with him. He was on his way to Baltimore from Washington. I went to the last-named
city and found his name on one of the hotel re-
gisters; but it stood alone, and without his place
of residence added."

As there existed no reason why Edgar should
not receive all the information about Edith which
we had to give, I said:

" We can help you in this."

" You can!" He became greatly excited, for
he saw that I was in earnest.

" Yes," I replied. " The object of your search
is in our immediate neighborhood."

" My Edith !"

" Yes, *your* Edith. Is it not so, Alice ? " I looked towards my wife.

" It is as my husband declares," she replied.
" I have known her, intimately I might say, for
months."

" You, Alice ! you know my Edith intimately
for months !" He turned to my wife, and catching
both her hands, held them tightly. Ripples of joy
were playing like sunbeams over his face. " Oh,
Alice, Alice ! "

" I know her, and love her, Edgar. And even
before you came, had from her own lips all the sad
story of her life."

" This is too much happiness ! " exclaimed the
agitated young man. " I shall lose myself. To

think that morning has indeed broken after such a night! But where is she?"

"You have seen Aunt Mary already?" said I.

"Where? when?"

"You saw her at the window of the corner house."

"And you knew it!" He turned his eyes flashing upon me.

"Yes."

"And led me away from the object for which I was in search?"

He spoke almost indignantly.

"For your own good and for hers also. The time had not yet come," I said calmly. "You were not in a state to be trusted with that knowledge."

"You were right, no doubt," he answered, as he drew a long, sighing inspiration.

"And she has told you all, Alice?" Turning to my wife he caught her hand again.

"Yes."

"All about our love?"

"Yes."

"Her heart is true to me still?" He bent nearer for the answer.

"True to you still, Edgar," she replied.

"Thank God! thank God! Hope, so long mocked, had lost faith in a day like this. But did Edith know that I was so near her?"

"She did not."

"Does she know of it now?"

"I think not."

"I must see her," he said. "The joy of our meeting shall be no longer delayed. Oh, Edith! Edith!"

He was losing himself.

"As you were calm in suffering, Edgar," said I, "so be calm in the blessing that is now about to crown your life. The mind of Edith has been greatly shocked. There have been periods when reason wavered. We have had anxious care on her account; but she is in a better state now. Do not disturb that state by communicating your own disturbance. When you meet her let it be as a strong man, against whom the waves of her weak feelings may break and be bounded. She will need all your wise as well as loving care. Think of Edith, and of what will be best for her. It would be a sad thing to lose her now."

"Lose her now!" He grew pale, and asked, huskily, "What do you mean?"

"The shock of excessive joy is sometimes fatal to reason," said I. "Edith must be guarded from all sudden excitement. She does not yet know that Alice is your cousin, and had better first be told of this. Then the rest can be gradually communicated."

How strangely is human prudence, and all its

wise forecast, sometimes set at naught! Even as I said this, the door of the room in which we sat conversing, was pushed open, and Edith came in with her almost noiseless step. We had not heard her light ring. She stopped a pace or two in the room, seeing a stranger. I did not utter her name, nor did a word fall from my wife's lips. We were in too much surprise and anxiety to speak.

"Edith, darling!" Edgar did not start forward, nor say these two words in a wild throbbing tone. He only moved towards her with a quiet step; and his voice, though unspeakably tender, was low and calm. She stood still—still as if life had ceased instantly.

"The night has departed, Edith!" He took her hands, and kissed her, oh, so gently! so placidly!—yet so lovingly!"

"We have both prayed for this hour, love, and it has come at last; and God make us thankful."

He drew his arm around her, still looking into her eyes. We stood apart, silent, motionless, and in tremulous fear. She only gazed into his face.

"Mine!" He said the word softly.

I saw a motion on her lips, and a flash of feeling in her eyes.

"Mine, for ever!" His voice was just a little tenderer—not in the least excited.

Now her hands were raised, and she placed

them on his shoulders. I saw the dead calm of her face begin to break up; I saw light coming into it.

"Oh, Edgar!" A smile glinted on her lips, as the words came forth.

His lips touched her lips again. I now perceived that he was trembling under the rush of feelings he was struggling to control.

My wife stepped forward, and with her woman's tact said, looking at Edith—

"Let me introduce you to my cousin."

In the surprise of that intelligence, as a new emotion, she hoped to save her from being borne down by other emotions, that were momentarily gaining power; and she was successful.

Edith looked away from Edgar's charmed gaze, into the face of my wife.

"My cousin," was repeated.

A gleam of pleasure, mingled with the surprise Alice wished to create, lighted up the countenance of Edith.

"My Edgar!" The happy woman laid her face down upon the young man's breast—not lost, not in wild bewilderment, not in tremulous agitation, but with a strange quietude of manner that I scarcely comprehended.

"Won't you send for Aunt Mary?" she asked.

My wife went for Aunt Mary and prepared her for the interview with Edgar. When she came in

Edith started forward, now for the first time losing herself, and throwing her arms about the neck
of her true-hearted relative, wept passionately for
several minutes. Then, the sunshine came out
after this rain of tears. I saw in the pale cheeks
of Edith, already, the faint signs of returning
warmth, the promise of summer roses. She had
passed through the shock of meeting with Edgar,
which we had feared, and was stronger and calmer. Her heart was already gathering up the se-
v red chord in the rending of which life had well
nigh perished.

" There's been something going on in that corner house," said our neighbor, Mrs. Watkins, calling over, as she did every now and then, on the
evening of this same day, "and for the life of me,
I can't make it out."

She had all along taken a lively interest in the
strangers at the corner, but as we had good reason for keeping our own counsel, Mrs. Wilkins
never found herself any wiser by researches in the
direction of our house. We, of course, took a
lively interest in what she had to say, because,
through her. we gained a knowledge of outside
impressions, and learned how near the truth of the
matter our neighbors were getting. They were
not very much wiser by what they could learn.

" What seems to be going on there ? " asked my
wife.

"Oh, everything that is mysterious. The peo·
ple about here are getting very much excited
about the matter."

"Indeed!"

"Yes!"

"What is exciting them?"

"I'll tell you, because I think you ought to
know. You've been seen going in there a few
times, and the two ladies in at the corner house
have been seen visiting you. As this is the case,
you should be apprised of just what people are
saying about them."

"What do they say?" we asked.

"It is said that the white-faced lady, Mr. Con·
greve's wife, has been guilty of a crime that ex·
pelled her from society in the West."

"I don't believe a word of it," said my wife.

"You'd better believe it, then," replied Mrs.
Wilkins. "I'm sure it's so."

"What else is said?" I inquired.

"It's said, that only a few nights ago, a carriage
was seen standing at the door, and that a man
came out of the house carrying a woman in his
arms, who was thrust into the carriage, he getting
in after her. The carriage drove off, no one at
tempting to stop it."

"Anything more?" I asked.

"Yes. A Mr. Congreve was killed on the rail-
road between Baltimore and Washington—Con·

greve is the name of the family at the corner house—and people say it's the corner house man. himself. But nobody has been brought there and there's been no crape on the door. I'm puzzled; I can't make it out. I suppose they were glad to get rid of him, and I shouldn't much wonder, judging him from his face."

Thus Mrs. Wilkins ran on; while we kept silent as to the true facts in the case.

A few days afterwards the lady came in to relate another story with which her husband had just furnished her. A customer from the West had given Mr. Wilkins nearly the true version the death of Mr. Congreve having revived in his mind the half-forgotten circumstances in the case

"But I don't believe a word of that," said Mrs. Wilkins, after finishing a pretty accurate narrative of what had really occurred. "It's too improbable."

The truth to her was stranger than fiction, and she fell back on the first story she had heard about the killing of a lover.

We encouraged her to believe in the true narrative; but she shook her head in obstinate doubt. It wasn't at all a likely tale, she averred. There were "too many ins and outs in it—too much risk involved. No man would be fool enough to lay such a trap for his own fingers."

So in our neighbor's eyes the mystery in the

corner house continued to be an unsolved problem. The closer intimacy which was now established between our families, and apparent to all, in no way lessened the curious interest that was felt.

"Who is the young man that's been staying at your house for some time?" asked Mrs. Wilkins, two or three months later in the progress of time. She had dropped in to talk with my wife.

"He is my cousin."

"Indeed! I wasn't aware of it."

" Yes."

Mrs. Wilkins looked a little surprised and a little mysterious.

" Do you know," she said, with some hesitation, as if she were making a communication that would not be altogether agreeable, "that he visits at the corner house frequently."

"Indeed!" remarked my wife.

"It's true, as I'm speaking."

" How frequently?"

" At least once every day, and sometimes twice. Mrs. Cromwell told me that she saw him going in there twice day before yesterday. I don't like to meddle in my neighbors' affairs, but I felt as if you ought to know about this. And now that I find the young man is related, I'm glad I've told you. He ought to be put on his guard."

My wife promised to speak with Edgar on the subject.

"Tell him," said Mrs. Wilkins, "that he'll get himself into trouble as sure as he's born. There's a mystery about them people; and where there's mystery, there's always something wrong."

"There's nothing wrong about our neighbor in the corner house," said I, coming in at this point, and speaking positively "There was something wrong, I have good reason to know, about Mr. Congreve. But he is dead, and the wrong is dead with him."

" What was the wrong? " asked Mrs. Wilkins, now all alive with curious interest.

" I can only answer that it was some disreputable, or I might say, criminal acts done years ago, and recently thrown open to light. But, in his death, has come a compensation for the wrong. It lay all with him, and died with him. The ladies are pure and innocent. Be assured of that, Mrs. Wilkins."

"Isn't there a murdered lover in the case?" asked our neighbor.

"Nothing of the kind," I replied.

She looked disappointed, for she had clung to that murdered lover from the beginning. It was a favorite hypothesis in explanation of the mystery.

"Then there isn't any great mystery after all," said Mrs. Wilkins, with evidently failing interest.

"The matter rests about where I have placed

it. Mr. Congreve, in pursuing some desired object, went, as other men often do, beyond right, justice, and humanity; and in his payment of wrong's sure penalty, suffering came to those who were in close connexion with him."

"They might have buried him decently," said Mrs. Wilkins, "if only for decency's sake." She grew a little indignant.

"His body lies in Green Mount Cemetery," I replied.

"Why wasn't it brought home? I never heard of anything so unfeeling! I don't think much of any woman who could treat a dead husband after that fashion! Why, there wasn't even crape on the door!"

I did not argue this point with Mrs. Wilkins. To defend Mrs. Congreve on the right ground, would be to reveal more than I cared to bruit through the neighborhood.

Mrs. Wilkins went home with less heart in the case. But a month or two later, her interest was quickened into life again by seeing the pale lady, no longer in black, walking out, leaning on the arm of Edgar Holman. She had not been invited to the private wedding which took place a few days before.

The corner house and its inmates became once more objects of curious speculation among the neighbors. But as nothing further in the way of

mystery showed itself, and the people began to
go abroad like other folks, appearing at church,
in the street, and occasionally at public places,
curiosity died out for want of fuel to keep the
flame alive.

A year has passed, and the neighbors, as they
go by the corner house, no longer glance up at it
in a mysterious way, or look eagerly towards the
door if it happens to stand open. It has become
to them an ordinary house, and its inmates are
regarded as among our common people of the
times.

THE END.

T. S. Arthur's Popular Works.

These books are all gotten up in the best style of binding, and are worthy a place in every household. Copies of any of them will be sent, post paid, to any address on receipt of price by the publishers,

John E. Potter & Company,
Nos. 614 and 617 Sansom Street,
PHILADELPHIA.

TEN NIGHTS IN A BAR ROOM, and What *I Saw There.* A truly touching series of powerfully-written Temperance sketches, which have proven a great auxiliary in the cause of reform, and have contributed largely to the author's great popularity. By T. S. Arthur. With Illustrations. Cloth. $1 25.

ADVICE TO YOUNG MEN on their Duties *and Conduct in Life.* Intended to strengthen their good purposes, to elevate their minds, and to educate them into sounder views than are common to the masses of society. By T. S. Arthur. Cloth. $1 25.

ADVICE TO YOUNG LADIES on their Duties *and Conduct in Life.* Designed to inculcate right modes of thinking as the basis of all correct action, and to eradicate the false views of life which everywhere prevail. By T. S. Arthur. Cloth. $1 25.

***THE OLD MAN'S BRIDE; or, The Lesson of
the Day.*** Showing the fatal error committed by those who, in disregard
of all the better qualities of our nature, make marriage a matter of bargain
and sale. By T. S. ARTHUR. Cloth. $1 25.

***THE HAND WITHOUT THE HEART; or,
The Life Trials of Jessie Loring.*** Exhibiting a noble and true woman,
who, during the bitter years of an unhappy marriage, swerved not amid
the most alluring temptations from honor and duty, and showing the final
reward of her long trial of faith, love, and high religious principle. By
T. S. ARTHUR. Cloth. $1 25.

***GOLDEN GRAINS FROM LIFE'S HAR-
vest-Field.*** Remarkably entertaining and lively pictures of actual life,
which demonstrate the importance of good principles, pure affections, and
human sympathies full of the soul's nutrition. By T. S. ARTHUR. Cloth.
$1 25.

THE GOOD TIME COMING. Exhibiting the dis-
satisfaction and yearnings of the human heart, and pointing out the golden
sunlight which from the distance is continually shining down upon it for
the purpose of warming and nourishing it. By T. S. ARTHUR. With Mezzotint Frontispiece. Cloth. $1 25.

***THE ALLEN HOUSE; or, Twenty Years Ago
and Now.*** Portraying vividly the legitimate fruits consequent upon the
pursuit of either of the two ways in life, the right and the wrong. By T. S.
ARTHUR. Cloth. $1 25.

WHAT CAN WOMAN DO? In which the great influ-
ence and power of woman, for good or for evil, is shown in a very interesting series of life pictures. By T. S. ARTHUR. With Mezzotint Frontispiece.
Cloth. $1 25.

THE WITHERED HEART. Affording a striking illustration of the necessity for avoiding the false and selfish principles which too often lead to a sad and total waste of being. By T. S. ARTHUR. With Mezzotint Frontispiece. Cloth. $1 25.

THE ANGEL AND THE DEMON. A work of thrilling dramatic interest, which contains moral lessons of the highest importance to families and young mothers, and which stands forth pre-eminently among the author's many fine productions. By T. S. ARTHUR. Cloth. $1 25.

THE TRIALS AND CONFESSIONS OF A *Housekeeper.* Furnishing, from real life, many of the trials, perplexities, and incidents of housekeeping, embracing in its range of subjects such as are grave and instructive, as well as agreeable and amusing. By T. S. ARTHUR. With Illustrations. Cloth. $1 25.

AFTER THE STORM. A new and fascinating volume in which the folly of too much reliance upon one's own opinions, and a disregard of the attentions due one another, is fearfully apparent, while the story is deeply interesting throughout, and the moral unexceptionable. By T. S. ARTHUR. Cloth. $1 50.

THE WAY TO PROSPER, *and Other Tales.* Showing the power of virtue, harmony, and fraternal affection among members of a family in securing their future well-being and prosperity, and, wherein the want of these qualities conduces to misfortune and ruin. By T. S. ARTHUR. With Mezzotint Frontispiece. Cloth. $1 50.

THE ANGEL OF THE HOUSEHOLD, *and Other Tales.* In which we learn how kind feelings and obedience to our better impulses benefit us, and how, with the little heavenly visitant, the tender babe, angelic influences enter the household. By T. S. ARTHUR. With Mezzotint Frontispiece. Cloth. $1 50.

TRUE RICHES; or, Wealth Without Wings, and Other Tales. The lessons in this work show how ruin succeeds to unfairness, and success to honesty of purpose ; setting forth truths that all should remember, and that no one can learn too early or too often. By T. S. Arthur. With Steel Frontispiece. Cloth. $1 50

HEART HISTORIES, and Life Pictures. Giving painfully correct histories, such as too often cloud the hearts of people and may generally be seen in the dreary eyes, the sober faces, the subdued and mournful tones that almost daily cross our paths. By T. S. Arthur. Cloth. $1 50.

HOME SCENES: Its Lights and Shadows as Pictured by Love and Selfishness. Directed toward keeping the light of love forever burning in our dwelling, and toward aiding us in overcoming those things which are evil and selfish, while each moral presented seems in itself a jewel worthy a place in memory's casket. By T. S. Arthur. Cloth. $1 50.

SPARING TO SPEND; or, The Loftons and the Pinkertons. A book showing the beneficial results of a wise restriction of the wants to the means—a virtue which all should possess, and which in this extravagant age cannot be too forcibly illustrated. By T. S. Arthur. Cloth. $1 50.

LIGHT ON SHADOWED PATHS. Stories which faithfully point to many of the different shadows that have crossed the paths of others, and which afford much of invaluable instruction, tending to rend the clouds that may hover o'er us, and to keep us within the sunshine of life. By T. S. Arthur. Cloth. $1 50.

OUT IN THE WORLD. Unveiling the sad experiences that necessarily await jealous, proud, and sensitive young men, and undisciplined, wayward, and petulant young women ; also, revealing the true and only way of escape. By T. S. Arthur. Cloth. $1 50.

OUR NEIGHBORS IN THE CORNER House. A fascinating and stirring narrative, which adds its terrible evidence to the fact that sin will find people out, and that justice will triumph over injury—even under extraordinary circumstances. By T. S. Arthur. Cloth. $1 50.

NOTHING BUT MONEY. Picturing, in the most forcible style, the difference between avaricious and ambitious men and those who prefer social happiness and peace; also, offering a striking lesson to the very many young minds in which gold outlustres every other consideration. By T. S. Arthur. Cloth. $1 50.

WHAT CAME AFTERWARDS. A sequel to the preceding volume, yet a story complete in itself, in which we are shown how the precious gold in our natures, after we have encountered severe discipline, will reveal itself in our intercourse with the world. By T. S. Arthur. Cloth. $1 50.

THE THREE ERAS IN A WOMAN'S LIFE; or, the Maiden, the Wife, and the Mother. A work depicting the happy effects of right training when brought in distinct contrast with the wrong, and showing also the fruits of right living. By T. S. Arthur. With Frontispiece. Cloth. $1 50.

BEFORE AND AFTER MARRIAGE; or, Sweethearts and Wives, and Other Tales. Drawing choice pictures of lovers and husbands and wives, faithfully contrasting marriage and celibacy, and teaching the folly of employing money to the mere pampering of pride and indolence. By T. S. Arthur. With Frontispiece. Cloth. $1 50.

THE MARTYR WIFE, and Other Tales. A remarkably interesting work, pointing out social follies, and including the excellent and popular stories of "The Heiress," and "The Ruined Gamester." By T. S. Arthur. Cloth. $1 50.

MARY ELLIS; or, The Runaway Match, and
Other Tales. Attractive experiences that will readily commend themselves to the real life of many who have sought for but never found their ideal. By T. S. ARTHUR. Cloth. $1 50.

THE YOUNG LADY AT HOME. Home stories most happily drawn by the author, involving the troubles, errors, and perplexities incident to domestic life, and showing woman's real mission. By T. S. ARTHUR. Cloth. $1 50.

STEPS TOWARDS HEAVEN; or, Religion in
Common Life. A volume, free from sectarian or denominational influences, which cannot but deeply impress the mind, and awaken in every one the highest type of human happiness. By T. S. ARTHUR. Cloth. $1 50.

LIGHTS AND SHADOWS OF REAL LIFE.
Containing a series of captivating and intensely interesting Temperance stories, which, perhaps, no other author can furnish with equal acceptance, and containing a moral suasion which cannot but affect for good all who read. By T. S. ARTHUR. With Illustrations. Cloth. $1 75.

SKETCHES OF LIFE AND CHARACTER.
Pleasantly written stories, drawn from everyday life, and free from all exaggerations, which invariably leave a powerful impression upon the mind of the reader. By T. S. ARTHUR. With Illustrations. Cloth. $1 75.

LEAVES FROM THE BOOK OF HUMAN
Life. A choice selection of stories, intended to leave the mind active with good purposes and kindly sympathies—the value of each one of which is clearly evident. By T. S. ARTHUR. Numerous Illustrations. Cloth. $1 75.

SWEET HOME; or, Friendship's Golden Altar.
A companion for the evening hour; pure in morals, elevating in tone, cheerful, hopeful, and reverent in all its views of God, and a transcript of "Home, Sweet Home." By FRANCES E. PERCIVAL. With Mezzotint Frontispiece. Cloth. $1 25.

THE ANGEL VISITOR; or, Voices of the Heart. Intended to bring light and joy to those who are heavy in heart, as well as to echo the gentle teachings of Jesus, and to comfort the sick and afflicted everywhere. By FRANCES E. PERCIVAL. With Mezzotint Frontispiece. Cloth. $1 25.

THE MORNING STAR; or, Symbols of Christ. An excellent volume, designed to magnify the beauty and wisdom of the Word of God, and to cause the believer and unbeliever to think more of the Saviour. By WILLIAM M. THAYER, author of "Hints for the Household," "Pastor's Wedding Gift," etc. etc. Cloth. $1 25.

THE SPIRIT LAND. An instructive and very desirable work, which is submitted to the public with the counsel that we cling to the Word of God as the only infallible guide of faith and practice amid the fanaticisms of the day. By S. B. EMMONS. With Mezzotint Frontispiece. Cloth. $1 25.

THE DESERTED FAMILY; or, The Wanderings of an Outcast. A forcibly and prettily written story, designed to soften the heart to just influences, to warm the affections to proper emotions, and to elevate and fructify the soul. By PAUL CREYTON. With Illustrations. Cloth. $1 25.

FASHIONABLE DISSIPATION. A stylish and brilliant narrative, which, together with "*Adela Lincoln: A Tale of the Wine Cup,*" included in the book, is high-toned and worthy popular favor. The former by METTA VICTORIA FULLER, the latter by M. F. CAREY. With Frontispiece. Cloth. $1 25.

LIVING AND LOVING. A collection of beautiful sketches which evince all the vigor, freshness, and attractiveness so peculiar to the authoress, and which are highly instructive. By VIRGINIA F. TOWNSEND. With fine Steel Portrait. Cloth. $1 25.

WHILE IT WAS MORNING. One of the authoress's sweetest stories, in which we are taught that sorrow, pain, and disappointment must come to all in the world; yet the grand truth stands out in glorious significance—"The righteous shall not lose their reward." By VIRGINIA F. TOWNSEND. Cloth. $1 25.

ANNA CLAYTON; or, The Mother's Trial. A tale of real life, written with beauty and force; and in its plot and execution of the very highest moral excellence and useful tendency. By Mrs. H. J. MOORE. Cloth. $1 25.

THE CHRISTIAN'S GIFT. Embodying some of the most select religious articles from the finest minds, among which are "The Refuge from the Storm," "The Sabbath and Heaven," "Heaven Conceivable to the Christian," etc. etc. By Rev. RUFUS W. CLARK, author of "Heaven and its Emblems," etc. etc. Cloth. $1 25.

WOMAN'S MISSION AND WOMAN'S IN-*fluence.* A wonderful work, of which Bishop Doane has said, "It is the very book which, if I had a thousand daughters, I would put into their hands, with the Bible and Book of Common Prayer, as their best companion, &c." Tenth American, from the Seventeenth London Edition. Cloth. $1 25.

THE ENCHANTED BEAUTY, and Other Tales, *Essays, and Sketches.* Embracing many of the finest, most elaborate, and finished articles of the well-known author. By Dr. WILLIAM ELDER, author of "The Life of Dr. Kane," etc. etc. Cloth. $1 25.

THE RAINBOW AROUND THE TOMB; or, *Rays of Hope for those who Mourn.* A carefully arranged and attractive book of selections, both of prose and poetry, containing much of wisdom in several departments, and forming a valuable and desirable gift for the Christian parent, child, or friend. By EMILY THORNWELL, author of "The Ladies' Guide to Perfect Gentility," "Young Ladies' Own Book," etc. etc. Cloth. $1 50.

HEAVEN AND ITS SCRIPTURAL EM-
blems. A series of articles on the splendors and joys of glorified saints
and their secret communion with the Father in the Holy of Holies. By
Rev. Rufus W. Clark, author of "The Christian's Gift," "Lectures to Young
Men," etc. etc. With Steel Illustration. Cloth. $1 75.

THE YOUNG LADIES' OWN BOOK. An offer-
ing of love and sympathy, dedicated to the maidens of her native land, and
containing admirable selections, in prose and verse, which will universally
be regarded as superior in quality and authorship to most similar works.
By EMILY THORNWELL, author of "The Rainbow around the Tomb," etc. etc.
Cloth. $1 75.

SUNLIGHT AND SHADOW; or, The Poetry
of Home. A sprightly and well-written work, in which we are led through
scenes and incidents descriptive of rural life in America; designed for the
entertainment of young men and ladies. By HARRY PENCILLER. Cloth. $1 75.

THE ORPHAN BOY; or, Lights and Shadows
of Humble Life. This touching story of humble life illustrates the magnet-
ism of love over the human soul, and in tho perusal of it the heart of the
reader will often be drawn out in sympathy with the hero of the tale. By
JEREMY LOUD. Cloth. $1 75.

THE FORGER'S DAUGHTER; or, Out of the
Shadow into the Sun. A book for pleasurable and profitable pastime,
which will interest and arouse the sympathies of every intelligent reader.
By MARTHA RUSSELL. Cloth. $1 75.

OUR PARISH; or, Pen Paintings of Village
Life. A delightful story of rural life, in which the principal characters are
among those earnest and sincere souls that gather every sabbath in simple
country churches. By GEORGE CANNING HILL, Esq. With Steel Frontispiece.
Cloth. $1 75.

OUR FOLKS AT HOME; or, Life at the Old Manor House. The object in this work is to impress upon the young the importance of having an object in life, and that object a really useful one. By EDWARD TOLIVER. Handsomely illustrated by engravings from original designs. Cloth. $1 50.

HANS THE STRANGER, and Other Stories. In which the author keeps in view utility in its higher sense, and endeavors to show to the young that the true purpose of life is not amusement or enjoyment, but usefulness. By EDWARD TOLIVER. Handsomely illustrated by engravings from original designs. Cloth. $1 50.

THE WREATH OF GEMS. A neat unique gift book for the young of both sexes, in which are selections from the best English and American literature—groupings which will be, doubtless, both new and highly acceptable. By EMILY PERCIVAL. Steel Frontispiece. Cloth. $1 50.

THE EARLY MORN. A small volume addressed to the young on the importance of religion, which will be found admirably adapted to such intelligent and educated young persons as have been unmindful of the demands of religion. By JOHN FOSTER, author of "Essays on Decision of Character." Cloth. 25 cents.

A full descriptive Catalogue of these and all our publications, including a great variety of Bibles, Testaments, and Albums, and embracing many of the choicest Biographical, Historical, Practical, and Miscellaneous Books in the country, will be sent to any address on application. Address,

JOHN E. POTTER & CO., Publishers,

614 and 617 Sansom St., Philadelphia.

www.ingramcontent.com/pod-product-compliance
Lightning Source LLC
Chambersburg PA
CBHW020941120726
47905CB00008B/2628